JOHN WAINWRIGHT
THE
TENTH INTERVIEW

By the same author:

Who Goes Next?
The Bastard
Pool of Tears
A Nest of Rats
Do Nothin' Till You Hear from Me
The Day of the Peppercorn Kill
The Jury People
Thief of Time
A Ripple of Murders
Brainwash
Duty Elsewhere
Take Murder...
The Eye of the Beholder
The Venus Fly-Trap
Dominoes
Man of Law
All on a Summer's Day
Blayde R.I.P.
An Urge for Justice
Their Evil Ways
Spiral Staircase
Cul-de-Sac
The Forest
The Ride
Clouds of Guilt
All Through the Night
Portrait in Shadows

JOHN WAINWRIGHT
——— THE ———
TENTH INTERVIEW

St. Martin's Press
New York

Library of Congress Cataloging in Publication Data

Wainwright, John William, 1921–
     The tenth interview.

     I. Title.   II. Title: 10th interview.
PR6073.A354T46   1986   823'.914   86-13866
ISBN 0-312-79120-8

First published in Great Britain by Macmillan London Limited.

First U.S. Edition

10 9 8 7 6 5 4 3 2 1

MAN TALKING

It came as a shock to realise that I was seriously considering the pros and cons of poisoning Norah. Nor was it one of those 'wouldn't it be nice' thoughts – one of those 'I wonder if' fantasies. It was a deliberate contemplation of various methods and choice of poison.

I hadn't even been thinking about her.

A couple of holidaymaking teenagers visiting the shop had acted suspiciously, in that they'd stared at the display of suntan lotions while, very obviously, eyeing the ceiling corner where the convex mirror reflected most of the display units to whoever was behind the counter. I could almost see their minds working and, when they strolled towards the sunglasses, I knew they'd realised that that was the one corner not reflected.

I had stepped to the poison cabinet. From there I could watch them through the gap between the shelves of gents' toiletries and baby foods and, in order to justify my presence in the dispensary, I'd raised my hand to the door of the poison cupboard.

My eyes had watched the teenagers, but my mind had been with my fingers; with the assortment of listed drugs and poisons behind the locked door. I knew exactly where they all were and exactly how much stock I carried. Quite suddenly, I realised the ease with which it would be possible to . . .

One of the teenagers slipped a pair of sunglasses into the hip pocket of his jeans.

I called, 'Hey, there!' and, as I moved, they ran from the

shop and turned right along the promenade.

'What is it?' The assistant joined me at the door, guessed what had happened and pointed. 'There they are. Turning up by The Beaconfield.'

'Leave it.'

I guided her back into the shop.

'But shouldn't we call . . . ?'

'No.' I answered the question before it was fully asked. 'They're away. The police haven't a hope of catching them.'

She looked mildly disappointed, but accepted my decision without argument.

I returned to the dispensary and prepared for the daily rush of customers. It was past five o'clock, and the patients with their prescriptions from the two nearby surgeries always built up before we closed at six. In short, it was a normal working day, other than that very positive thought; the thought that it might be possible to poison my wife without the risk of detection.

I pushed the thought aside as I busied myself. Preparing prescriptions calls for a high degree of concentration.

When the last capsule had been counted and bottled, when the assistant had left and I'd closed and locked the door and I was in the dispensary preparing things for the next day's work, I once more allowed my thoughts to toy with the near-forbidden subject.

I tried to be logical. I asked myself blunt questions, and tried to find truthful answers.

What was my reason for wishing to poison her? What was my reason for wanting her dead?

In short, what was my motive?

On the face of things there was no single, simple motive. Instead, there were a thousand tiny motives, none of which could be pinpointed as anything more than a minor irritation. The demand that I always wear a tie. 'Herbert, there is a basic standard of dress. If you fall below that standard you

8

become slovenly.' The refusal to understand my interest in philately. 'Herbert, little boys collect stamps. Not grown men.' The never-ending series of convenience-food meals. 'It's much fresher. They fast-freeze it *immediately*. It's also much quicker to prepare.'

Annoyances, then, but not motives. Not *motives*! But so many of them, and for so long.

We had been married twenty-six years, and we had a daughter who a couple of years before had, herself, married and who now lived here at Rogate-on-Sands, less than a mile from her old home.

In retrospect, I think Jenny had made it bearable. She had been the balm on a festering sore. But now the balm was no longer there, and the tiny stabs of irritating pain plagued unhindered.

And yet . . . .

I allowed myself a wry smile when I reminded myself that Norah was a *good* wife. Oh, yes. Ask her, and she would tell you. Indeed, given the opportunity, she would tell you without being asked. She was a good wife, who never looked at another man, who could turn a house into a home, who could bake better than most wives, was thrifty, could sew a little and converse about things that were not too complicated. She was clean. Clean about the house, clean about her person, clean in her language. She was all these things, therefore she was faultless.

And, indeed, she was.

Via the measuring rod of her Women's Institute and Town's Women's Guild friends, whom she regularly invited to our home for coffee and gossip, she *was* faultless.

I stood with my hands on the top rail of the promenade and looked out to sea. The tide was in, the sun was setting and, as always, it was quite beautiful. The ragged-edged path of saffron leading from the setting sun and across the foam-flecked ripple of an unusually quiet Irish Sea.

'The Golden Road to Samarkand.'

Years ago – a lifetime ago – we'd both stood near this spot and watched this same magnificence. Teenagers, unspoiled by the grime of living. We'd gazed out at the same sun, across the same sea and, simultaneously, we'd both uttered the same words.

'The Golden Road to Samarkand.'

Nor had it been one of those near-impossible coincidences that pop up now and again through life. We attended the same grammar school, and were in the same class. The last lesson had been English Lit., and we'd touched upon Flecker. His phraseology and use of imagery in *Hassan* had been discussed. Then we'd left the school grounds together, walked home via the promenade and paused to watch the sun being quenched far out on the sea's horizon.

'For lust of knowing what should not be known, We take the Golden Road to Samarkand.'

That, I think, was the first time I became aware of her. I'd noticed her, of course, but only as a fellow-pupil. I knew her father was a local accountant and she, in turn, knew my father was one of the Rogate-on-Sands pharmacists. But that's about all we knew. That, and our respective names.

From that moment we seemed to grow nearer. Not close. At least, not until much later. Nevertheless, our lives seemed to run alongside each other and, very gradually, to converge, until we became friends, then confidants.

When it happened – when it became accepted that we'd eventually marry and spend our lives together – it's impossible to say. I suspect it was hinted at and, perhaps, even taken for granted, but there was nothing definite until I'd completed my training, was a qualified pharmacist and was working alongside Father in the shop.

Thereafter, it became an understood thing. Our parents were friends, therefore we were friends and everybody was delighted when we became officially engaged and, a year or so later, married. There was no passion. No great and consuming love. On our wedding night we were both virgins and counted that not at all unusual.

I make neither pretence nor apology. All my life I've been a dull dog. At best an introvert and shy – even standoffish – with strangers. When pressed, I've described myself as a 'loner', but the more accurate word might have been 'alone'. Even 'lonely'.

And yet, in the beginning and for those first few years, we found great tranquillity in each other's company, and that seemed to suffice. What we neither of us realised was that tranquillity and boredom are near-neighbours, and that boredom can spawn evil thoughts which, in turn, can lead to evil deeds.

Rogate-on-Sands is, I suppose, and by modern standards, a rather douce holiday resort. Its population is around the 40,000 mark and, come May, there is a gradual build-up of visitors which peaks in August, then tapers off to the residential figure by the end of September.

All my life I have lived here, and all my life I have loved the place. It is what a quiet, pleasant holiday resort should be, but rarely is. It has a delightful stretch of beach, but no donkeys and few buckets and spades. There are no rock stalls, no shellfish stalls and no candy-floss stalls. It aims for a certain result by catering for a certain class of person, and it achieves that result, and few residents complain.

It boasts one three-star hotel – The Beaconfield – half a hundred lesser-classed hotels and countless 'guest houses'. It is a place favoured by the retired well-off; a quiet spot in which to end a not-too-tiring life. Equally, it is a place where less rumbustious people seek short periods of relaxation from the rat-race. It has its fair share of 'residential homes', and streets of massive, Accrington-brick-built houses, many of which have been converted into modern, well-appointed flats. It also has quiet drinking spots in which simple, but nicely presented, 'pub lunches' are served.

This is Rogate-on-Sands, and Norah and I were as much a part of it as Rock Walk, or the tiny Victorian pier.

I walked home from the prom that evening, and I was sad. In effect I was already a moral murderer. My mind was made up, and all it now needed was the act itself. I now find it strange – even terrifying – that having reached the decision, I never once had second thoughts. Norah was going to die, because I was going to poison her.

Nevertheless, the certainty made me act a little strangely. Every few steps I stumbled slightly, I seemed to have difficulty in keeping my mind concentrated enough not to bump into passing pedestrians and my eyes were a little out of focus. The feeling was on a par with being ever so slightly drunk. Indeed, I stopped a couple of times and took a few deep breaths and, for a moment or two, it seemed to help, but the vague wooziness soon returned.

Norah was not at home, nor would she be until at least nine-thirty. The local amateur operatic society's production of *The Yeomen of the Guard* was in rehearsal and Norah was some sort of backstage functionary.

There was a meal of sorts waiting on the kitchen surface. One of those tinfoil-wrapped 'immediate dinners' from the freezer cabinet of the local grocer. That, and a bottle of English perry masquerading as a table wine.

I didn't mind. I'm no gourmand, nor ever was. I read the instructions on the packet, popped the tinfoil tray into the oven, then went for a quick shower.

I ate the meal from the work surface of the kitchen. I can't even remember what it was, much less its taste. I drank the perry – the whole bottle – but it was much like drinking water.

Then I went into the lounge, poured myself a weak whisky, consulted the *Radio Times* and tried to watch a documentary which sounded interesting. I couldn't concentrate, and the effort to try to concentrate merely irritated me. I switched the television off, sat in the gentle gloom given

12

off by a standard lamp, sipped my drink and allowed my thoughts complete freedom of movement.

In the beginning we shared this common love of music. In those days the radio, not television, was our prime source of home entertainment. An occasional visit to the cinema. A concert, at least once a month. A shopping expedition to Manchester, ending at a concert given by the Hallé Orchestra. Sometimes an evening trip to Blackpool – out of season, of course – to hear some other great orchestra at The Opera House, or The Grand. And Rogate-on-Sands had its own musical society with visiting chamber ensembles.

Music, then. But, as time progressed, I realised that our tastes in music differed. Or perhaps we moved apart musically, too.

Operetta stretched her taste to its limits. Offenbach and Johann Strauss the younger were as far as her appreciation would go. Musical comedy and 'Palm Court' music was, I discovered, what she enjoyed most. The music bored me, but I went along. I was prepared to sit through frivolity for the sake of marital harmony. I did not (and still do not) count the music from *The Student Prince* as a vocal and instrumental Everest, but Norah did and I was content to let her have her way.

She refused to reciprocate.

My gods were Brahms, Beethoven, Tchaikovsky with, occasionally, a little Stravinsky. I never tired of the Mozart operas and Verdi, at his best, could bring my nape hairs up on end.

There was this great gap in our musical appreciation and, although I tried to bridge it, Norah never pretended to be other than bored by what suited me.

But, having said all that, a differing taste in music is no reason for murder.

Had Jenny still been with us . . .

Jenny I loved, and still love. Before she had a name –
when she was a tiny, closed-eyed bundle in a maternity
hospital cot, at the foot of a bed – I loved her more than I'd
ever loved anybody before, and more than I've ever loved
anybody since. She was Norah's child. Our child. But she
was *my* Jenny.

After her birth I wanted no other children. Some men
yearn for a son, to perpetuate their name. I find that both
foolish and arrogant. What 'names' are *worth* perpetuating?
What families are so important that without them the world
would be less complete? I wanted no son. Jenny was reason
enough for my having lived.

As she grew I tried to make her into a complete person.
Not just a complete woman . . . a complete *person*.

I tried to teach her toleration and benevolence and if that,
coupled with my present story, seems to smack of hypocrisy,
I can only say that I succeeded. She went to the school Norah
and I had attended, and she did well without being brilliant.
She was an outdoor person and in that she was unlike her
parents. She had friends galore and, even when they tended
to be rowdy, I found little difficulty in smiling my pleasure at
Jenny's happiness.

That was when Norah's interest in the various women's
organisations began. At first I think it was an excuse for
leaving the house when Jenny brought her friends home.
Then, gradually, she grew to know the clique of Rogate-on-
Sands wives who were members of those organisations. The
'glossy magazine' readers whose interests I find petty and
shallow. The mothers and wives who act out their roles for
the benefit of themselves.

They have a shallowness I could never understand.

I could, I suppose, have joined the male equivalent
societies, but I never wanted to. I knew the men – the
husbands of Norah's friends – and sometimes we talked when
I visited a local pub for a quick lunch. They bored me, with
their loud-mouthed bonhomie, their bragging and their

never-ending tales of business and fornicatory conquests.

I comforted myself with the knowledge that *I* had Jenny.

I stood aside and watched her grow. Marvelled as she slowly blossomed into a teenager and, perhaps, became a little sad when she matured into a young woman. I suffered the agony of every father when she reached the 'dating' age. This, I realised, was the testing time. The time when all I'd taught her – all the second-hand experience I'd gently brought to her attention – would either be acted upon or ignored. The temptations were there. The inducements to over-indulge, to experiment, to try out new experiences. When she was eighteen (and in the face of some opposition from Norah) I gave her a key to the bungalow.

'You make your own decisions now, my pet. For good or evil. If you need advice, we're here to give it. If you make a wrong decision – and you'll *make* wrong decisions, because we all do – we'll still be here. No recriminations. No fault-findings. Only comfort and love. Somewhere to run to, when you're hurt.'

Later, when we were alone, Norah criticised.

'You should have waited a few years.'

'I think not.'

'Until she was of age. Until she was twenty-one.'

'They're of a different generation, Norah. Eighteen *is* "of age", these days.'

I won't say she wished I was wrong. She, too, loved our daughter. But I know she worried. She lacked my unqualified faith in Jenny. She loved her less than I loved her. Far less than I loved her. . . .

THE INTERVIEW

I

'Why the devil . . .' shouted the detective chief inspector. Then he closed his mouth, breathed heavily through his nose and sat down at the Interview Room table. He stared across at the man sitting opposite him for a moment, then, in a much quieter and more friendly tone, said, 'Why the devil didn't you just divorce her, and have done with it?'

'On what grounds?'

'Incompatibility. I don't know. Walk into any solicitor's office and ask. It isn't my line of business, but I get the impression that divorce these days is about as easy as buying a television licence.'

'She wouldn't have agreed.'

'You think she *would* have agreed to your poisoning her?'

'No. Of course not.'

'You're crazy. D'you know that? You're quite crazy.'

'No.' The man shook his head. 'With you people – with the police – it's all black or white, but life isn't like that. Most of life is grey. Sometimes a light grey, sometimes a dark grey. But grey. It's compromise. That's what life is . . . a series of compromises.'

'You poisoned your wife?'

The man nodded.

'Deliberately, and cold-bloodedly?'

'Deliberately, but not cold-bloodedly.'

'My friend . . .' The detective chief inspector seemed to have difficulty in making his point. 'Murder by poisoning is the most deliberate form of taking life I can think of. Of them all, it's the most premeditated. The rigmarole leading up to it. The decision about the poison. The business of administration. There's a dozen opportunities – a *hundred* opportunities – to have second thoughts, but *you* didn't. You didn't! You went right ahead and poisoned her. That, by any yardstick, is cold-blooded.'

'By your yardstick,' smiled the man. 'But yours is a very short yardstick. A very limited yardstick.' He paused, then added, 'I didn't hate her, you know.'

'What?'

'I didn't *hate* her. I merely disliked her. I wanted to leave her as much dignity as possible . . . in the circumstances.'

'You *killed* the bloody woman. If what you're telling me is true. . . .'

'It's perfectly true.'

'You *murdered* her.'

'And if I'd divorced her? Assuming there'd been a way – some form of legal chicanery – if I'd divorced her?'

'She'd be alive today.'

'That would have been cruel,' said the man solemnly. 'To have divorced her would have been very cruel.'

'I don't get it. I don't follow.'

'The various women's organisations she was a part of. What would they have said behind her back? And she'd have known. She wasn't a fool. She'd have known, and it would have hurt her beyond words.'

'So-o,' mocked the detective chief inspector, gently, 'you poisoned her out of kindness?'

'I chose the lesser of two evils. She was a lonely woman, Chief Inspector. That, too, had to be taken into consideration.'

20

'Lonely! All these clubs, institutes, guilds?'

'They weren't her friends. Only acquaintances. She had no *friends*. She was like me. She couldn't make friends easily. They were acquaintances, therefore they would have mocked her. If we'd divorced, I mean. As it is, they "remember" her, without contempt. She isn't laughed at. She isn't sneered at.'

Jenny made everything possible. When Norah and I grew bored with each other – when we'd reached the point when simply to be in each other's company for any length of time became a burden – Jenny made it bearable. She was like balm on a wound and, when she married, the balm was removed. The wound festered and spread. Drastic surgery was needed.

And yet, despite our own difficulties, I think we were good parents. By silent but mutual agreement we never bickered in front of our daughter. She never knew the strain of our marriage.

It wasn't too difficult. Most days I was away at the shop. Most evenings Norah was away at her various women's groups. Sunday, we all three went to morning service at church, then, in the afternoon, Norah napped for a few hours while I retired to my study and busied myself with my stamps. Jenny had her own room, of course, and, what with homework, her record-player, entertaining her friends and watching her own choice of programme on the tiny TV set I'd set her up with, as a family – as a *complete* family – we were rarely a threesome.

The holidays were the most difficult times. I limited them to a fortnight each year plus, of course, Christmas, Easter and the various Bank Holidays. But those fortnights were a strain. They were a strain on Norah, too . . . they must have been.

I recall one year. Jenny was twelve years old, and one of her schoolfriends had spent a holiday on the canals. Jenny was keen, and it seemed a good idea. A peaceful holiday, chugging from inn to inn, watching the countryside glide past while we relaxed and forgot the rat-race of everyday life.

Great God!

Within the confines of that boat, with comparatively primitive washing and cooking facilities.

'I feel filthy.'

'Mummy, it's exciting. It's different.'

'It's disgusting. It isn't even civilised.'

22

'Norah, dear,' I soothed, 'that is part of the holiday. To get away from "civilisation". To take things easy.'

'I don't like bunk-beds. I don't relish the thought that we might have rats on board somewhere.'

'Mummy, they're only water rats. Haven't you read *The Wind in the Willows*?'

'Of course I've read *The Wind in the Willows*. But that doesn't mean I like toads, or rats or even moles.'

'Mummy, have a sense of adventure,' Jenny pleaded.

There was a small landing-stage ahead and, before Norah could do more damage, I steered the boat to starboard and said, 'There's a public house and a tiny shop there, Jenny my pet. I think I'd like some barley sugar sweets. Nip ashore and get some, please.'

I waited until Jenny had left the boat, then I turned on Norah.

'You're ruining the child's holiday,' I accused her.

'What about *my* holiday?'

'You don't count.' It was the first time I'd put it so bluntly, but we hadn't much time. 'Jenny is enjoying herself. To her this is a great adventure. Whether *we* are enjoying it isn't important. Personally, *my* enjoyment is seeing my daughter happy.'

'You're soft. You can't see that . . .'

'No, I'm not soft.' I spoke quietly, but she knew I meant every word. 'But be warned, my dear. If you're not prepared to tolerate a little discomfort – if you complain or whine any more – you'll be left at the next inn, to make your own way home.'

'You wouldn't dare.'

'You have my solemn assurance,' I warned her.

'And what about Jenny? What will she say?'

'She'll be told you've suddenly remembered an appointment. With one of your groups. With the Institute or the Guild. Something urgent that you *must* attend.'

It could have developed into a protracted argument – a

blazing row, perhaps, except that we didn't *have* blazing rows – but our firm rule was *never* to squabble in the presence of our daughter.

The rest of the holiday was quite a success. Jenny enjoyed herself, and that was the only thing of any importance.

It was after I'd decided to poison her that I realised how fortunate I was. Fortunate as a pharmacist, I mean. The business had been started by my grandfather. My father had taken over and I'd assisted until his death and now, though at times it was something of a drudge, I was able to keep things going without employing more than one full-time and one part-time assistant to deal with the counter trade.

Over the years we'd built up a business beyond what could be offered by the chain-store chemists. Inland from Rogate-on-Sands, but still part of Prem Valley Borough Council, there is much first-class farmland. There is enough animal husbandry to keep two veterinary practices busy. Add to that the 'secret' remedies beloved of farmers themselves and the near-witchcraft potions hawked by ancients who claim to know the mysteries of animal ailments, and you will realise that *my* poison cabinet was no mere store-cupboard in which to pack the drugs listed in the Monthly Index of Medical Specialities.

Veterinary medicines, for example, are dangerous. Some of the mixtures capable of curing a sick horse can kill a mere human in a matter of hours. Some of the contents of home-made rat poisons have to be handled carefully, wearing surgical gloves. I know at least two farmers who, rightly, diagnosed foot and mouth disease in their cattle – *and cured it* – without the appropriate ministry suspecting a thing. At a guess, I was the only pharmacist within a radius of twenty miles able to supply the ingredients required for that cure.

Nevertheless, I keep a very tight rein upon the drugs in my possession. My Poison Register is kept meticulously, and no poison leaves the shop without it having been signed for.

My father had kept the same poisons, and for the same reason. It was he who had installed the poison cabinet. Fairly shallow, but as capacious as a moderately sized safe, it is of good steel and securely bolted to the wall of the dispensary. It is fitted with a Chubb lock, and only I have a key.

I had the poisons, then. I merely had to decide which one to use.

Then, having decided to poison Norah, I spent hours trying to convince myself that I *shouldn't*!

It was rather like having an aching tooth, then visiting the dentist. The pain goes. At the very least, it seems to ease. Logic insists that it *hasn't* gone and that without a filling or an extraction it will continue to give pain, but the self-delusion continues.

I recalled the day Father died. We'd been close. More like friends than father and son. Perhaps my being an only child had helped but, for whatever reason, we'd had no secrets from each other.

One afternoon, about a week after we'd announced our engagement, he said, 'Herbert, you're sure Norah will be the right wife for you?'

'Of course. That's why we became engaged.'

He was measuring the ingredients for a liniment at the time. He kept his eyes on the measuring-jar, but a gentle and rather sad smile touched his lips.

'Do you have doubts?' I asked.

'Not if you don't.'

'But you *have* doubts,' I insisted.

'You're very much *like* each other.' He stopped pouring and re-corked the container.

'Surely that's to our advantage.'

'Like can live with like,' he agreed. 'But opposites – assuming there's good understanding – seem to have a better chance.'

'But we don't *need* "understanding", Father. We already understand each other perfectly.'

'That's all right, then . . . isn't it?'

He had his back to me as he made the murmured remark. He was replacing the container to its place on the shelf.

Nothing more was said. Indeed, there seemed nothing more *to* say. As I saw things he was merely an affectionate father who happened to be feeling a little sorry for himself at the forthcoming marriage of his only son.

At the wedding he was obliged to make a short speech, thanking those who had come for coming, and wishing us happiness. He did it well. No silly jokes or innuendoes, just a general expression of appreciation, plus the hope that Norah and I would make a go of it.

Little more than two years later – less than two months before Jenny was born – he died.

He'd have loved Jenny. He'd have loved Jenny very much. They both had a certain common *honesty*. A basic decency which is rare. Very rare.

I found him unconscious, in the store-room. It was stock-taking time and he'd left me in the pharmacy while he listed what we had and what we needed. He'd been gone longer than I'd expected and, thinking he might need some help, I'd climbed the stairs to the store-room. He'd had a massive heart attack and was sprawled on the floor alongside the cartons.

He was in a coma for less than twenty-four hours, then he died. There was the business of a post-mortem and an inquest, then the funeral arrangements.

He'd been an old-fashioned man and, perhaps, set in his ways and beliefs. To him, cremation had always been not quite 'Christian'. On the few occasions we'd touched on the subject he'd mentioned a 'decent burial' in the local churchyard.

That's what I had in mind and that, I'm sure, is what Mother expected.

Norah argued, 'It's very unhygienic.'

Mother murmured, 'I think it's what he'd have wanted.'

We were in the bungalow. Mother had come to stay with us until the immediate distress had eased a little. It was that dark, helpless period between a death and a funeral; a time of ever-present memories mixed with a terrifying dread of the future.

I grant that Norah had been carrying Jenny for more than six months. It made her scratchy and forever on the point of tears. That, or always wanting to argue.

She said, 'It's nothing to do with me, Mother-in-law, but *I'm* going to be cremated. You're never at peace, otherwise.'

'He's dead, dear,' mother sighed. 'He's already at peace.'

'Churches don't last forever.'

I stared. For the moment, I couldn't understand her.

'They fall down,' she explained irritably. 'If the council want to widen a road, they make compulsory purchase orders, and graveyards become part of the highway. If that doesn't happen, they get weed-choked. Churchyards are *always* miserable places.'

'He didn't go to church often,' said Mother, gently. 'But when he did he enjoyed it.'

'That's no argument against cremation, Mother-in-law.'

'All right . . .' I tried to push aside the great weight of sorrow. Tried to be logical. 'If he's cremated. He *still* has to be buried.'

'It doesn't follow.'

'For God's sake!'

'Herbert, your father loved the Lake District. It was where he planned to retire.'

'I don't see what . . .'

'Scatter his ashes. Let him end up where he *wanted* to end up.'

Which is why, about ten days later, I found myself a passenger in a rowing boat, on Ullswater. I had the ashes in a bag. A plastic bag. All that was left of my father, in a cheap, plastic bag and, when the boatman rested his oars, I tipped the contents over the side.

That was when I last saw my father. Not when the curtain was drawn around the coffin. When I saw a film of dust spread on the surface of the water, then slowly sink and disappear. *That* was when I said goodbye.

Just me and a strange boatman. I think Mother would have come, had I asked her. But I didn't ask her. Indeed, I insisted that she *shouldn't*. The strain would have been too much.

Norah couldn't come, of course, even had she so wished. She was very much pregnant, and becoming more trying by the day.

I watched the last of the stain sink into the dark water and, quite suddenly, realised what it meant. A father who, in his own way, had been a great man. One of my few friends. And now, no gravestone. No marker. Nowhere to visit and remember.

Nothing!

Mother stayed with us until after Jenny was born. It wasn't done deliberately, it just happened. Those last few weeks, before the birth, saw great and unnecessary traumas.

Unless something goes wrong, childbirth isn't an illness. It's not a 'complaint'. It's not an 'injury'. Indeed, from what little I'd heard or read about the subject, women are expected to experience a great realisation. The textbooks all say they 'blossom' . . . whatever that may mean.

I would argue with those textbooks.

Perhaps it was a difficult birth. It was certainly 'difficult' for me. Mother, on the other hand, was helped through what could have been a very wretched period of her life. She hadn't *time* to mourn. She fetched and carried, washed and scrubbed, from morning till night. Nor did she seem to mind.

One evening, when Norah had decided to go to bed earlier than usual, I apologised.

'I'm sorry, Mother,' I mumbled.

'Whatever for?' Her surprise was quite genuine.

'I don't want you to feel you're being made use of.'

'Of course I'm being made use of.' She smiled. 'I *want* to be made use of. It shows I'm still wanted.'

'You know what I mean, Mother.'

'Herbert.' She leaned forward and touched my arm, as if sharing a secret. 'Norah's frightened. *I* was frightened. That's not unusual. Your father, God rest his soul, was quite useless. Most men are. But she'll have her baby, and she'll be happy again. She'll be even happier than she was before. And you'll be proud. Especially if it's a boy. . . .'

II

'You're back-tracking a bit.' The detective chief inspector scratched a match into flame and lighted a cigarette. He made no move to invite the man to help himself from the opened packet on the table. 'Your daughter's a married woman. You're going back to before she was born. Why?'

'It's all part,' whispered the man.

'Part of what?'

'What I've had to go through.'

'You think you're unique?' The detective chief inspector tilted his head and blew cigarette smoke at the Interview Room ceiling. 'There are times when I could swing for *my* old lady. I doubt if I'll poison her.'

'You don't understand.'

'I don't even believe you . . . yet.'

The man gawped his incredulity.

'We get nutters,' smiled the detective chief inspector.

'I'm not mad.'

'Of course not. None of them are.'

'You think I *am* mad?'

'You're either mad, or you're a murderer. I don't know which. I'll decide . . . eventually.'

'I poisoned my wife.' The man's tone moved towards desperation. 'I had reason. Not one reason, a hundred-thousand reasons. I didn't *want* to poison her.'

'Ah!' The detective chief inspector drew on the cigarette.

'What does that mean?'

'Not deliberate. Accidental.'

'Of course it wasn't accidental.'

'If you didn't *want* to poison her?'

'I'm putting it badly,' groaned the man.

'I get the gist.'

'I poisoned my wife. Believe me, *I poisoned my wife.*'

'Because she talked you into having your father cremated?'

'That was only one thing. One of a great many.'

'Hardly motive for murder?' smiled the detective chief inspector.

'That's what I'm telling you. That's what I'm trying to get across. There wasn't a "motive", as you call it. Not one thing you can put your finger on.'

'Let me put you straight, friend.' The detective chief inspector leaned forward a little. He rested his elbows on the table and spoke quietly and with gentle earnestness. 'We don't *need* a motive. Means and opportunity . . . that's all. The rest is trimmings. *Res gestae*. That's the flash name for it. The name the lawyers use. So – OK – you had the means. For sure you had the opportunity. Those things aren't at issue. You get the problem? I'm not too interested in "why?". But I'm very interested in "whether?".'

31

Had there been another way, I wouldn't have poisoned her. Had there been any other way!

Divorce was out of the question. I was determined to leave her as much dignity as possible. I couldn't just walk away and out of her life. I had the shop to consider and had I merely left I might never have seen Jenny again.

Outwardly, I suppose we were looked upon as a happily married couple moving gently, if a trifle sedately, through our middle years. We never quarrelled in public. Indeed, we rarely quarrelled at all. In retrospect, I think we lacked enough emotional involvement with each other to really quarrel. Indifference was the keystone to our way of life. Indifference, with a façade of respectability. We had a few acquaintances, but no real friends. An occasional invitation to dinner and an evening's chat was the limit of our mutual social life, and those occasions were rarely a success. There was no discussion, because discussion equated with argument and neither of us liked to argue.

I think the everlasting plateau of dreary mediocrity was at least one reason why I had to rid myself of Norah. Not that I wanted excitement. I merely wanted *change*. Something that ensured that I didn't know exactly what I'd be doing this time next week, this time next month . . . even this time next year!

It was not too far removed from solitary confinement and, as the realisation grew, I began to wonder.

How many others? How many couples behind those chintz curtains, beyond those well-kept lawns? How many married and shackled by the gyves of 'respectability'? How many never-ending lies being lived?

For a short time it became a game. Watching the men and women I knew – the apparently happily married couples – and seeking signs of their *true* relationship. And, because I sought, I found. The man who offered simple courteousness to strangers – who said please and thank you, or stood aside to allow another woman to pass – but didn't do these things for his wife. The woman who, when speaking to a strange man, did so with a smile; whose tone of voice differed from that she used when speaking to her husband. It wasn't flirting. It wasn't even trying to impress. It was just that they, too, were trapped in the same squirrel-cage and, like me, could find no reasonable way out.

Oh yes, I saw them. In the shop. At lunch, either in a pub or in a café. When they asked a question, or gave an answer. When they answered the telephone.

I even wondered how many had contemplated murder.

I certainly saw it in Norah, and toyed with the idea that she might even have considered the idea of murdering *me*.

I toyed with the idea of various poisons. Having reached the decision and despite the nagging half-doubts I think I realised that the final drastic step had, at some time, to be taken; therefore I considered the various advantages and disadvantages of what I had at my disposal.

Strychnine was by far the quickest, although not quite as immediate as is popularly thought. The timing is in minutes rather than seconds and, if the dosage is badly miscalculated, can even be as long as an hour. I had no desire to prolong suffering, and that, too, was a major consideration. Vaquier had used it in the mid-1920s. So had Dr Palmer, who had administered it with brandy. But these and the others had been evil, insensitive men. I wasn't like them. I merely wanted Norah out of the way. I didn't want to *hurt* her.

There was also, of course, the undoubted fact that a post-mortem examination would certainly have discovered traces of strychnine.

Palmer, Seddon, Maybrick, Crippen. I didn't want to be set alongside criminals like they were. I wasn't a criminal. What I intended was not for gain. It was not meant to remove Norah in order that I might go to some other woman. There was no 'dirty' reason for my wanting to rid myself of her. No shameful cause.

33

On the other hand, of course – and I'd be a fool to deny this – I was not anxious to end up in prison. I had a moderately prosperous business and, apart from the marital side of things, was a reasonably contented man.

Had she been more understanding – had she met me even part-way . . .

We had a great argument shortly after the birth of Jenny. It was, I think, our first real argument. The first time we met head-on.

Norah's parents had fluttered around but, in the main, had not been much help. Unlike my own mother they had merely voiced platitudes and done much to encourage Norah into believing that giving birth to a child was some form of near-fatal disease.

Mother had been of great assistance during the confinement, and for the first few weeks after Norah had left the maternity hospital. Even Norah admitted that.

'I don't know how we'd have coped, Mother-in-law.'

'That's all right, dear. It's helped me over a difficult period, too.'

'I don't know how I could have looked after Baby, *and* done the housework, *and* made Herbert his meals.'

I was there when the exchange took place. I could, of course, have reminded Norah that I always took lunch out, that I usually prepared what little breakfast I needed myself and that my evening meal, when I arrived home from the dispensary, amounted to little more than a snack. But, already, I knew that women like Norah only believe what they want to believe. Motherhood, to her, was a burden. Something to be 'suffered'. I held my peace.

Nevertheless, the day arrived when Mother dropped hints about returning to her own home.

'You'll be lonely,' I said, quietly.

'It will pass, dear. I think the worst is over now. Thanks to you and Norah.'

34

'And Jenny, of course.'

'Of course,' she smiled. 'And Jenny.'

That was all that passed between us but a few evenings later I broached the subject with Norah.

Mother had gone to bed. At least, she had gone to her room. Throughout her stay she had behaved impeccably. She'd recognised our desire for some period, each day, of personal privacy. It was her habit, therefore, to retire by mid-evening. Whether she went to bed, or whether she read a little before retiring, I don't know. But, whatever, by no later than eight o'clock, or thereabouts, she left us. Jenny had settled, until the small hours, and Norah and I had space in which to discuss things.

'I'm worried about Mother,' I said.

'Why?' Norah seemed genuinely unable to understand the remark.

'When she leaves here,' I amplified.

'She has a home to go to.'

'It will be a very lonely home, without Father.'

'Oh, I'm sure she's got over that.' She reached for a woman's glossy and flipped through the pages, apparently seeking some article which might interest her.

'Norah, I'd like to talk about it,' I pressed.

'What?'

'Mother.'

'What about her?' The magazine was open on her lap and the impression was that she was slightly annoyed at being interrupted in her search for something to read.

'I thought . . .' I paused, then said, 'Would you object to my suggesting to her that she lives with us?'

'I certainly would.' She closed the magazine.

'If only temporarily?' I compromised.

'Herbert, I'm not having another woman sharing my home.'

'She's not "another woman",' I objected. 'She's my mother, and she's very recently lost her husband.'

35

'Herbert, don't dramatise things,' she accused.

I stared.

She almost snapped, 'Surely even *you* aren't *so* blind. It hasn't actually broken her heart.'

'That,' I gasped, 'is a disgusting thing to say.'

'*I've* seen no sign of tears.'

'She hasn't worn her heart on her sleeve,' I raved, quietly. 'She hasn't made everybody within sight and sound share her misery. But that's because of what she *is*. Unlike you, she doesn't demand never-ending attention.'

'She's not coming to live here, and that's flat,' she said coldly.

'Don't *I* have a say in the matter?'

'No, you don't. You're out at your stupid shop all day. She wouldn't be under *your* feet.'

'You haven't complained about her being "under your feet" during the last few weeks,' I said, sarcastically.

'She's been useful.'

'Useful!'

'She's saved us money. If she hadn't been here we'd have had to employ either a nurse or a housekeeper.'

'For God's sake, Norah!' I allowed my temper to fly. 'You've given birth to one child. One. Not triplets. Not quadruplets. One child. Women do that with a whole family of other children, without half the fuss you've made.'

'A certain *class* of woman.'

'What on earth is that supposed to mean?'

'Herbert, let's get one thing straight. I have no intention of being a child-bearing machine. We might as well understand that from the start. I've given you a child. I have no intention of starting a whole dynasty. It wasn't an easy birth, but it's there.' She touched the cover of the magazine. 'The people who write in these things. They go on about "the maternal instinct". It's something I haven't got. Something I don't understand. I find changing its nappy a distasteful thing. These midnight . . .'

36

'"*It!*"' I blazed. 'Since when has our child been an "it"? She's a human being. She has a name.'

'Don't be tiresome, Herbert.' Her tone was heavy with mock world weariness. 'I'm prepared to accept your child without complaint. I'll do my best to be a good parent. But I'm *not* having the additional strain of coping with your mother. She has a home of her own. She can visit . . . of course she can. But she can't *live* here. Knowing her, I doubt if she'd want to.'

'Knowing *you*, I doubt if she'd want to.'

That was the first full-blooded argument. It took more than a week to get back to a more-or-less normal routine. It taught me something, too. In a face-to-face row I'd never be able to compete with my wife. Just below that well-brought-up exterior there was steel *I* couldn't hope to penetrate. What I'd once mistakenly thought to be shyness was, in fact, complete selfishness. Self-centredness, in fact. Until our original friendship had developed she'd kept herself to herself merely because she had an inbuilt contempt for other people.

That was the lesson that first argument taught me, and only very rarely did I forget that lesson.

As for Mother, she left for her own home within a week. I don't think Norah said, or did, anything to hasten her departure, but I suspect that our coolness towards each other upset Mother, and she was no fool. She could make educated guesses.

I visited her at least twice a week, usually on my way home. Just to call in and check that everything was as it should be. She, in turn, visited us about once every fortnight. For Sunday lunch, usually. She watched Jenny grow from a baby into a child, and there was a bond forged between them. Jenny loved her grandmother, and Mother fairly doted on her granddaughter.

Mother died about five years after Jenny was born.

* * *

37

So many times I've tried to understand that first quarrel with Norah. That first *real* quarrel, and the hurtful things she said. I'm not a complete fool. I know, and appreciate, that the first head-to-head argument after marriage can be – *must* be – a traumatic milestone. The last of the gilt is stripped from the gingerbread, and what is left is either suspect or everlasting. I think that *that* – not the marriage ceremony – is when the bond is either forged or broken.

I sought for excuses. I truly wanted my marriage to work. *Our* marriage to work. I knew enough about medicine to know of the so-called 'lactation period'. Even the law recognises this period of a woman's life. Those first few months, when some women are no longer in control of their emotions.

At first I used this as an excuse. An excuse for Norah. But it was a very empty excuse, and eventually I knew that, too.

Go far enough back, and the real reason is my own stupidity. My own inexperience with women. With girls, when I'd been in my teens. I had hopelessly misjudged the girl I'd asked to marry me. I'd known no other girls, therefore I had no matrix against which to measure her. Otherwise I might have recognised the signs. The breaking of dates, with no hint of excuse. The selfishness with which she insisted that we go where *she* wanted to go, or see films *she* wanted to see. The convenient 'headaches' which were used as a ready-at-hand reason for bouts of unnecessary petulance.

That first quarrel was a little like the raising of a curtain to reveal a well-lit stage in what had previously been a darkened auditorium.

Jenny was at school, and she was beginning to enjoy school. She could read, she could do a little arithmetic and she was obviously a very intelligent child.

Then Mother died. Jenny's beloved 'granny'.

A visiting neighbour found her in a bad way, sent for an

ambulance, then telephoned me. I rushed to the hospital and, about two hours later, was with her when she died. It was a peaceful death. The sort of death she deserved. But that didn't make it any easier.

That evening – it was a beautiful summer's evening – Jenny wanted to visit her granny.

'You can't, pet,' I said, gently. 'She's ill.'

'She's dead,' added Norah, and it was said without passion. Perhaps without meaning to hurt and perhaps without thought.

'What's "dead"?' Jenny looked first at her mother, then at me. There was complete non-understanding in her expression. She asked, 'When will I be able to visit her again?'

'You won't, my darling.' It was breaking my heart, but I held out my arms and Jenny came to me, for comfort and explanation. I chose my words with infinite care. 'People become ill, Jenny. When they're old ladies – like Granny – they sometimes die. That means they don't get better. They go to sleep, for ever. That's what being "dead" means, pet. Going to sleep, and not waking up.'

'Not even when I shake her?'

'No, my pet,' I choked. 'Not even when you shake her.'

The child didn't understand. What child of that age *can* understand? But later, when she'd gone to bed and I'd called in to touch her forehead with my lips and check that she was asleep, I made mild protest to Norah.

'I think you were a little cruel,' I murmured. 'A little harsh.'

'The child has to know these things.'

'No innocence?' I think I smiled and, if so, it was a sad smile. 'No fairies? No stars?'

'I dislike half-truths.'

'Even when they're white lies, told to cushion hurt?'

'Herbert, your mother – Jenny's grandmother – is *dead*. I'm not glad . . . don't think that. But neither am I a hypocrite. She's not "ill". She's *dead*. The child must be

39

taught the facts of life.'

'And of death . . . presumably?'

'And of death,' she replied.

'She'll not end up in Ullswater,' I muttered. 'Not there. Not this time.'

'That's your decision.' She really didn't seem to care. About the death of Mother. About me. About anything. There were a few moments of silence, then she stood up from her chair. 'I think I'll go for my bath. After what's happened today, I feel like an early night.'

There was a funeral. This time, a burial in the churchyard. I was the only member of the family present. Norah made some empty excuse which I made-believe to accept, and Jenny was too young and wouldn't have understood. Just the funeral people, a bored-looking cleric, a couple of Mother's neighbours and myself.

It was a poor ending to a good and quietly lived life and, as the coffin was lowered, the combination of grief and guilt almost choked me. Hers was to be a particularly lonely grave. She wasn't even joining the man she'd loved.

That night I moved into the spare bedroom.

Why that night?

Just that it seemed appropriate. We'd slept in separate beds since the birth of Jenny. It was no additional hardship to sleep in separate bedrooms.

Norah made what I suspect was only token protest.

'We shall be without a spare bedroom.'

'I'll get the study rigged out with a bed-settee. I'll rearrange things within the next few weeks.'

'It's your decision. Let *that* be understood.'

'I know.' I smiled. 'Even *I* make decisions, sometimes.'

'And what if friends come? What if they want to stay the night?'

'What friends?' I parried. 'We *have* no friends. People who call at this house don't stay overnight.'

It was a small mutiny, and a small victory. It added up to nothing – *meant* nothing – in the mounting derision for each other that was taking over our lives. . . .

III

'Cyanide,' murmured the detective chief inspector.

'I beg your pardon?'

'Cyanide.' The detective chief inspector screwed what was left of the cigarette into a cheap, tin ashtray advertising 'Players Navy Cut'. 'The Nazi crowd liked it. It's quick. *Very* quick.'

'Hydrocyanic acid,' said the man, with some annoyance, 'is not only quick. It's very painful. Good heavens, man, we're talking about *prussic acid*.'

'You've already talked about strychnine.'

'And dismissed it, because it produces prolonged pain.'

'And, of course, because it can be traced?' smiled the detective chief inspector.

'So can cyanide. You don't even have to open up the body. The smell of bitter almonds lingers. . . .'

'So, *that's* why?' teased the detective chief inspector.

'What?'

'Pain doesn't really come into it. It's whether the damn stuff can be traced or not. That was the main consideration.'

'You're a fool,' snapped the man.

'One of us is.'

'You can't understand – or *won't* understand – the problem I had to face. I had to rid myself of her, but I'm not inhuman. I didn't want her to suffer.'

'Very laudable,' mocked the detective chief inspector.

The man was genuinely indignant when he asked, 'What do you think I am?'

'If you're telling the truth —'

'Of course I'm telling the —'

'— a psychiatrist's dream boy. He'd have you on the couch for hours.'

The man took a long and shuddering breath, then whispered, 'I'm not mad, Chief Inspector.'

'No?' The raised eyebrow was derisive.

'I came here. I wasn't brought. I *came*.'

'Of course.'

'I wasn't arrested. I came to this police station in order to confess.'

'This is an interview room. Not a confessional. If you're seeking some strange brand of absolution . . .'

'I'm not!'

'My friend.' The detective chief inspector's tone moved smoothly to a more friendly disposition. The ghost of a smile played at the corners of his mouth as he spoke. 'Among other things – among many other things – I'm paid to listen. *You* pay me. As a rate-payer, as a tax-payer, you're the one who helps me draw my salary. Not vice versa. That's why I'm listening. That's why I'm sitting here, wondering what the hell this is all about.

'A particularly dominating wife? That's *your* side of it, of course. A doting father? Well, all fathers tend to dote on their daughters a little. That doesn't make you unique. That doesn't even surprise me. A whimpering, weak-kneed husband? That comes across, of course. That comes across with all bands playing and all flags waving.

'But a poisoner? A murderer?' The detective chief inspector allowed the pause to stretch, until the silence

43

seemed to scream. Then a full smile touched his lips, as he continued, 'The man you're describing – the man you've so far described – wouldn't have the guts to murder. Even if he wanted to – even if he was driven to the very edge – he'd draw back, at the last moment. He's a masochist . . . but doesn't know it. A whipped dog, drooling at its mistress's heels and waiting for the next taste of the lash.

'It takes courage to murder, my friend. It takes a very special sort of courage to murder in cold blood. And poisoning is the most cold-blooded way of them all. So much time. So many opportunities to have a change of heart. Crippen was a poisoner. Crippen was very much like you. A pathetic, laughable little nothing. Very much like the man you're describing – very much like *you*, if you're to be believed – but he had a woman behind him. Ethel le Neve. *She* was the strength . . . not Crippen.' The detective chief inspector paused, then, in an almost bored voice, asked, 'Do you have an "Ethel le Neve" tucked away somewhere?'

Contrary to popular belief, celibacy is not a difficult state to achieve. At first there are certain basic urges, but they wear off and, in time, what Sigmund Freud placed so high on his list of priorities is seen for what it is. Self-gratification, which can be denied without too much of an effort.

I reorganised my study. Indeed, I did rather more than reorganise it. It took almost a year to sell Mother's house and dispose of what property we didn't want. I let Norah decide upon which soft furnishings, which blankets and sheets, which cutlery, crockery and glassware she fancied. Then I chose a few pieces of furniture. My choice was determined more by memory and sentiment than by necessity and among the things I chose was the bed I'd slept in, prior to marriage. It was a good bed – a 'three-quarters'-sized bed – and I knew it to be very comfortable.

I placed it, and the few other bits and pieces I wanted, in storage, then approached a local architect.

Between us we drew plans and extended the study to more than twice its original size. We included partition walls, which in turn created a small bathroom, complete with shower and toilet, and what amounted to another bedroom. *My* bedroom, in which I installed my own bed.

I had bookshelves fitted to the walls of my new study. I bought a radio-cum-record-player. Not stereo. Not hi-fi. I was not technically minded enough to understand what was, in those days, the up-and-coming thing. All I required was books and music, and the privacy in which to enjoy them.

Norah was, I think, more annoyed than shocked.

'You certainly know how to spend money.'

'I'm not going into debt.'

'I just don't see the point of it all.'

'We've decided to live our own separate lives.'

'*You've* decided.'

'And you object?' I smiled, as I spiked her on her own quickly answered remark.

'It's your money.'

'It's *our* house. It's in both our names. At the very least it will add value to the property. What's the name they're starting to call them? Granny flats, isn't it? If we ever decide to sell, we can always call it a granny flat.'

'I hope you're happy in your "granny flat",' she sneered.

I didn't mind her contempt. I knew I *would* be happy . . . and I was.

Outwardly – beyond the walls of the house – we remained the same people. Apparently happily married. Quite normal. What very little socialising we did continued as before. An odd evening with acquaintances, but never more than once a month and, because we so rarely reciprocated by extending a return invitation, even those evenings out became fewer. We went to concerts, amateur theatricals and sometimes the cinema and, as before, we went together more often than not. Nobody seemed to notice the difference.

I learned a great truth. It is possible for a man and wife to be with each other, to smile and chat with fellow-creatures and yet, at the same time, each to ignore – even forget – the presence of the other. The men talk with the men, the women talk with the women. It is taken for granted – in our case erroneously – that a married couple are on amiable terms.

At home there was what I suppose might be termed 'armed neutrality'. There was a pattern. Other than my own quarters, Norah kept the house as clean and smooth-running as ever. My evening meal was waiting for me, although I usually ate it alone in the kitchen. The laundry was done and ready for use whenever I required and, by silent but mutual understanding, Jenny was never allowed to be aware of the cool toleration with which her parents lived their complementary lives.

I could have turned Norah during those first few years after Mother's death. 'Tamed her' is too strong a way of putting it, but I could certainly have rebuilt our marriage on my own terms.

I discovered that, unlike myself, she could only suffer her own company for a limited time. By mid-evening I was comfortably ensconced in my study, reading, listening to the radio or playing one of my records and, short of sometimes visiting the kitchen for a pre-bedtime snack, I was there for the night. I was up early next morning and away to the shop before either she or Jenny came from their rooms. I was content. Life had the very minimum of problems.

But one evening Norah knocked on the door and when I called she entered and for a moment seemed tongue-tied.

'Yes?' I asked.

'There's a television programme,' she said. 'I thought you might like to watch.'

'I don't like television,' I reminded her.

'It's a symphony concert. Mozart's "Prague".'

'I have it on a record.'

'Yes, I know, that's why . . .'

'I do not need some producer to switch cameras in order to emphasise that the violins, or the woodwind, have taken up the main theme. It's distracting. I prefer to just *listen*.'

'I – er . . .' I sensed she was virtually forcing the words out. 'I thought you'd like to sit with me.'

I raised the book I'd lowered, and said, 'I'm re-reading Thomas Hardy's *The Woodlanders*. I'm nearing the end. I'd like to finish it before I go to bed.'

I suppose it was an olive branch. I suspect it was meant to be. I had no qualms about rejecting it. Already I'd grown to like the comfortable solitude of my study. What happened in the rest of the house was not my concern. I was prepared to pay for its upkeep, ensure that neither Norah nor Jenny lacked whatever necessities, or small luxuries, they required but, in return, I demanded my privacy.

A womb-substitute, if you will, although I wouldn't have described it as such. To me it was a civilised withdrawal from

47

a life which, in a few short years, had given me as many kicks in the teeth as I was prepared to take.

Jenny came in, of course. Jenny had freedom to enter or leave my study as she wished. Indeed, when she sought privacy which fell a little short of the privacy of her own room, she would join me and either listen to music or read. I introduced her to books that I know she still re-reads with pleasure. First the 'Alice' books, then, perhaps a little painfully, Dickens – starting with *Hard Times*, which I guided her through virtually a chapter at a time – then Jane Austen and the Brontë sisters. By the time she was sixteen she knew the mysteries of good literature. She knew what the author was 'saying' behind the printed word.

But before that, Norah twice more tried to tease me from my self-imposed isolation.

'Herbert, I think we should get out more.'

This was about a month – perhaps a little more than a month – after the 'television' episode.

I turned the volume of the radio down a little, and waited.

'It's a glorious evening,' she commented.

It was. It had been a scorching day; we'd done a brisk trade in suntan lotions.

'A walk along the front,' she continued. 'Watch the sun setting.'

'Do I detect nostalgia?' I smiled.

'I'm sorry?' She looked puzzled.

'It's not important.'

'A walk along the promenade,' she pressed.

'Jenny would like that, I'm sure.'

'I mean us two. You and me.'

'Where's Jenny?' I asked.

'She's visiting one of her friends.'

'She might come back and find the place locked. She wouldn't like that.'

'She won't be back till nine. She said so.'

'Just a walk along the prom?' I made no move, neither to

switch off the radio or to leave my chair. I wouldn't deny that, in a perverse way, I was quietly enjoying myself.

'It's a lovely evening.' I thought I detected a hint of desperation in her tone.

'Are you so bored?' I teased. 'So bored with your own company?'

'Herbert.' Her attitude stiffened. Her eyes became a little colder and she became the old Norah. The Norah I wanted no part of. She almost snarled, 'I'm not begging. I'm not crawling. If you don't want a walk, I can find better things to do.'

'Good.' I nodded. 'You see – or perhaps you *don't* see – I watch the prom all day through the door of the shop. It holds no delights for me.' I paused, then added, 'Nor, come to that, do you.'

It took her a long time to forgive me that victory. That small success in our everlasting clash of hurt and counter-hurt. She'd lowered her guard a little too far and she never again repeated *that* mistake.

The next time it was an ultimatum, and that was a full two years later.

She walked, stiff-legged into my study and, without preamble, said, 'It's Mother's birthday tomorrow. They're throwing a little party at The Beaconfield. We're going.'

'We've been invited, have we?' I remember, I was reading *The Caine Mutiny* at the time, and was finding it particularly absorbing. Perhaps that's why I met her head-on.

'Of course we've been invited. Who else would they invite if not us?'

'You're interrupting my reading,' I pointed out.

'Damn your reading!'

'Damn your mother,' I retorted, mildly. 'If you recall, you refused to attend *my* mother's funeral. Why should I attend *your* mother's birthday party?'

'What sort of an excuse can I give? How can I . . .'

'Tell the truth,' I suggested. 'That I dislike your mother

49

only slightly less than I dislike her daughter.'

'You've waited a long time for this,' she stormed.

'I'm a patient man,' I agreed.

'If you don't go, I'll never forgive you. I'll do no more work for you in this house.'

'What will you live on,' I asked, 'when I stop your allowance?'

'I can go to court.'

'Ah, yes . . . but *will* you?'

I raised my book and continued reading. She ranted on for a short time, but I'd heard all I wanted to hear and said all I wanted to say and, eventually, she stormed from my study.

She went to the birthday party. So did Jenny. I didn't.

Norah didn't carry out her threat. There was some slight drop in the already cool temperature, but I hardly noticed it. For myself, I continued as normal . . . as, indeed, did Norah.

Courts are not there for 'decent' people and, to the rest of the world, we were that. Without actually being pillars of Rogate-on-Sands society, we had certain standards to uphold. Outside our private life we had built up a firm reputation of quiet prominence. The blue-rinse clique of the town already counted Norah as one of their younger members and she, in turn, was rather flattered.

Her husband?

Oh, he was a quiet old stick, pleasant but shy, and good for a moderate donation to any worthy cause for which they were collecting.

It was a web, you see. The sort of web found in all small townships like Rogate-on-Sands. My own parents had been part of that web and Norah's parents were still part of it. An apparently innocent way of keeping like in touch with like; of weaving a barrier against 'undesirables'; of making sure that visitors were never *quite* allowed into the private sanctums of the residents.

Innocent! Did I say *innocent*?

That web had strands of tempered steel. They all do. To be

50

caught in the mesh is to be subjected to its unspoken laws. That, or be rejected, and to be rejected is on a par to being excommunicated.

I make no claim to be an expert in anything other than my profession, but I had sense enough to know about that web, and the fact that Norah was self-centred enough to want to be part of that web. They counted for something, these 'genteel' institutions. They were important. They meant that you *mattered* in the town.

Norah didn't go to court. Norah did *nothing*. By this time, the web had entangled her and her personality was such that she couldn't – daren't! – break loose.

The truth is, of course, that whereas Norah acted instinctively, my actions were all very deliberate. Instinct had, perhaps, played some part in things at the beginning, but I soon realised that I could never beat Norah at *that* game. The trick was to play a waiting game, then be ready.

For hours – hundreds of hours – I'd pondered the problem in the silence of my study. How to subdue a shrew? Not the Shakespearian way, of course. I was not that sort of a man. But there was another, more subtle, way.

No woman likes to be ignored.

That was the first truism I discovered. Unlike other species, the *female* of the human race – at least of the so-called 'civilised' parts of that race – displays the finery. The clothes and the cosmetics. The hairstyles and the frilly underclothes. The everlasting pin-ups prove my point. They have a desire to attract attention. They flaunt themselves, in order to be noticed and, thereafter, to dominate.

Therefore, refuse to 'notice' them, and they are at an immediate disadvantage. They are like a man shadow-boxing on a trampoline. They are both off-balance and they are hitting nothing. But what *is* being hit is their ego!

Most women have venom in their tongues.

Very rarely is there a hell-or-high-water friendship

between women. The spitefulness is too near the surface. The bitchiness is never completely under control. They fight, where men would smile. They hurt, where men would forgive with ease.

Therefore, refuse to *be* hurt. Agree with them and in agreeing remove that at which they aim their spite. What they express is only an opinion, and only *their* opinion at that. Above all else, don't argue. To argue with an angry woman (and women only argue when they *are* angry) is as fruitless as throwing away a ball attached to your wrist with elastic. It returns, but from a different direction. Their argument is based upon 'intuition', which means it lacks logic and is rarely related to the truth. Facts – proven facts – are dismissed, or ignored, if they in any way weaken whatever proposition a woman puts forward.

Women are as carnally voracious as men – perhaps more so . . . and perhaps until they are older. Read the gossip columns. Take note that the society women bed-hop with all the animal enthusiasm of their male counterparts. The female pop stars who glorify in the description of 'raunchy'. Not for them the protest songs. The dirges about how lonely it can be in the small hours. Their forte is the heavily emphasised, hip-wriggling outpourings concerning their fornicatory prowess. And, in the audience, their sisters-in-sex scream their understanding.

Women are everlastingly curious about the lifestyle of the street-walker. So-called 'decent' women. They wonder 'how', they wonder 'why', they wonder 'how many times'. They are all prostitutes at heart!

Those were the conclusions I reached. They were the truths, via which I could deny Norah her domination over me.

IV

'All worked out,' drawled the detective chief inspector. 'Every "i" dotted. Every "t" crossed. I wonder you don't write a book on psychology.'

'What?' The man seemed to 'return' to the Interview Room. It was as if his mind had wandered off, then returned at the sardonic remarks of the detective chief inspector.

' "How to Handle a Woman" . . . as the song title says.'

'Not *all* women. Just Norah.'

'It sounded like blanket advice.'

'You won't take me seriously.' Annoyance showed on the man's face, and was in his tone. 'You think this is some – some . . .'

'Headline hunting?' suggested the detective chief inspector.

'It's not. I poisoned her.'

'Now, if *she'd* come in here and said she'd poisoned *you* . . .' mused the detective chief inspector.

'You look upon me as a fool,' said the man, sadly.

'I look upon you as a prick . . . since you ask,' said the detective chief inspector. 'A pompous little prick, too weak to accept that marriage – every marriage – has its rough spots.'

'Strong enough to poison her,' countered the man.

'You think that needs strength? To uncork a bottle? To pour – whatever it was – into her coffee? Into her tea?'

'Strength of character. That's what I mean.'

'Let us assume . . .' The detective chief inspector pushed his chair back and straightened. He pushed his hands into the pockets of his trousers and strolled, first one way then the other, as he spoke. At first he didn't even look at the man sitting at the table. 'Let us assume, purely for the sake of argument, that all this isn't some involved come-on. That all the spilled garbage I've been listening to is the truth. That in fact you deliberately chose to live the life of a hermit. A very comfortable hermit, though. No sackcloth and ashes for you, my friend. A womb-substitute, that's what you've called it, but a very luxe womb-substitute. Central heating. Comfortable chairs. All the books you need. A radio and a gramophone. Even your own bathroom and bog. If you *must* opt out of life, do it in style . . . wouldn't you say? Shelve your responsibilities with a certain flair.'

'It wasn't my choice. It wasn't . . .'

'It was!' The detective chief inspector stopped his pacing, stood to one side of the man, and let the man have the full force of his contempt. 'By God, it *was* your choice. *You* built the extension. The "granny flat" as you call it. *You* sat there, on your tod, listening to your music. Reading your books. Working out all this steam-heated understanding of women. You fed, you were watered, you were laundered. All you did was sit on your pathetic little arse and feel sorry for yourself. *That* was the choice and, if you're to be believed, *you* made it.'

The outburst silenced the man for a moment, then, having regained what little control he'd lost, the detective chief inspector resumed his seat and once again lighted a cigarette. Again he made no move to offer the packet to the man.

'OK,' said the detective chief inspector, heavily. 'You're there, tucked away in your own little private haven. Putting on some sort of front for the neighbours, presumably?'

'We've never been very gregarious.'

'But sometimes?'

'Very occasionally we went out together.'

'Everything on the up-and-up?'

'On the face of things.'

'With some difficulty, surely? In view of the state of play at home.'

'We acted out our charade. I've explained. Most people do. It's all rather easy, when it has to be done.'

'Holidays?'

'Apart from my honeymoon, I've rarely taken a holiday since Jenny was a child.'

'And your wife and daughter?'

'Until Jenny married, they went together. At least once a year.'

'And since then?'

'Norah had a month in Harrogate last year.'

'That must have given her a new lease of life.'

'Chief Inspector, I'm not here to . . .'

'I know.' The detective chief inspector waved an impatient hand. 'You're not here to talk frivolities. You're here to confess to murdering your wife.'

'Quite.'

'And I'm here to be convinced.'

'What exactly does that mean?'

'It means,' said the detective inspector grimly, 'that you're either a nutcase, or the most egotistical bastard I've ever met.'

'Because I poisoned her? Because—'

'Egotistical. Self-opinionated. Cold-blooded. And, maybe at the same time, utterly spineless. You, my friend, are a mixture completely new to me. I thought I'd seen them all. But you're in a class apart.'

I decided upon aconite.

I knew enough of the substance to realise that, of all poisons, it was the most readily obtainable to a person in my position. It is part of so many old-fashioned remedies. Remedies favoured by country people and the farming communities.

My training as a pharmacist had taught me that aconite is obtained from the dried root of monk's-hood. A vegetable poison which, more often than not, causes cardiac failure.

To be quite sure, I consulted textbooks on toxicology. Eaton's book on famous poison trials. Glaister's *Power of Poison*.

I recall one lunchtime. I'd decided which poison to use, and had left the neat little café where I'd enjoyed a light meal. There were at least fifteen minutes before the shop was due to re-open, and I walked slowly along the promenade, then sat in what I thought was an empty shelter, looking out to sea. My intention was to collect my thoughts upon my chosen means of ridding myself of Norah. Of seeking any weaknesses that might have escaped my attention.

The shelter was partitioned into four separate compartments, and the division was of fairly thin, warped boards. In the next compartment were three people. Two women and a man. They were obviously elderly people, on holiday. The man was apparently the husband of one of the women and, as so often happens at holiday resorts, a conversation had been struck up with the second woman who, it would seem, was a stranger. I couldn't help but hear the conversation, if only because the man was hard of hearing.

One of the women – the woman not married to the man – said, 'We've picked a lovely week.'

'What?' The other woman answered.

'A lovely week. It's only rained on one afternoon. I think we've picked the best week of the year.'

'We've been here a fortnight. We're going back tomorrow.'

I tried to tune out the conversation, and concentrate upon the poison.

Aconite. Sometimes called aconitine. From the plant monk's-hood, sometimes called wolf's-bane. The leaf looks like parsley and the root looks like horse-radish. A plant once beloved of witches and, supposedly, having an effect – and sometimes a counter-effect – upon vampires and werewolves. A very ancient poison. A poison steeped in superstition and ancient mysticism.

'We're from Leeds.' The man's voice was loud and penetrating. The voice of a deaf man who believed everybody else suffered his affliction. 'Headingley. It's part of Leeds. Where the cricket ground is.'

'We have a cat, you see,' the second woman explained. 'He'll be missing us.'

In a booming voice, the man echoed, 'We have a damned cat, otherwise we'd stay on.'

'He doesn't like it.' The second woman added further, unnecessary explanation. 'He says it smells, but it doesn't. And they know, y'know. Animals. Animals know when people don't like them.'

The Romans used aconitine. So did the Greeks. It was called 'The Stepmother's Poison' in those days. It was used extensively. It was even grown, quite deliberately, for that purpose. Wolf's-bane. It became so widespread that an edict was proclaimed forbidding Romans from growing it in their gardens.

'We're going home tomorrow,' boomed the man. 'By train. We change at Preston.'

'Blackpool,' corrected the second woman.

'Eh?'

'It's that hearing thing.' The second woman's voice gave weary explanation. 'I keep telling him, but he won't have it seen to.'

A toxicologist called Christison once refused to name the poison, aconitine, when giving evidence. He wrote the name down and passed it to the judge. At that time, there was no known way of tracing it in the human body after death. It is still almost impossible to detect . . . unless, of course, it is deliberately looked for.

The man said, 'We change at Preston. It's a mucky station, Preston. You never know where owt is.'

'Blackpool,' corrected the second woman, sadly. 'We changed at Preston coming. We change at Blackpool going back.'

Thus the stupid argument formed a backcloth to my thoughts. The argument about some unimportant cat. The argument about Preston and Blackpool. Shallow people, wasting time indulging in shallow argument and being foolish enough to count it as 'conversation'.

But a great deal happened before that. A *great* deal.

Jenny was about twelve years old – no more than thirteen – when I discovered that Norah had developed a habit of visiting my study while I was away at the shop. I had nothing to hide, you understand, but it *was* private. It was on a par with *me* fishing through the contents of *her* handbag, without her knowing. It was an invasion, and I objected to it.

As I recall, I made the discovery because one of her hairpins had fallen onto the carpet. Jenny didn't wear hairpins, and certainly *I* didn't.

When Jenny had gone to her room to do her homework, I took the offending hairpin from my pocket and held it out.

'Yours?' I asked.

'Yes. Of course.' She took it from my palm and placed it on a side-table near her chair.

'I found it in my study,' I said. 'On the carpet.'

'Oh!'

'Why were you in there?' I made it a mild enough question.

'Checking that everything was clean and tidy.'

'And was it?'

'Of course.'

'Norah,' I reminded her. 'I have never yet asked you to dust or clean my quarters. The rest of the bungalow should keep you well occupied. *My* quarters are *my* concern.'

'They're clean enough,' she admitted with reluctance.

'Naturally. I'm methodical and I'm tidy. That's all it needs. The rest is merely a run-over with a duster and the vac, and an occasional touch of furniture polish. More and more women are proving that being a housewife is *not* a full-time job.'

I'd recognised her excuse for what it was. Quite empty. She'd been curious. Inquisitive. Even prying. She had refused to accept the fact that a man can keep a few rooms in order without the constant assistance of a woman, and proof that I *could* irritated her.

Nor was there anything I didn't want her to see. I had no hidden passion for pornography. No secret diaries. All I wanted was privacy. But complete and uninterrupted privacy, without qualification. It seemed so little, yet she refused me even that.

I had the feeling that she continued to snoop around when I was at the shop, and I set out to prove it.

One day I positioned my blotting-pad on the desk surface with absolute accuracy. I carefully measured the corners of the pad from points on the desk top. Then I slid a sheet of plain paper under the pad, but left enough exposed to ensure that anybody with an inquisitive turn of mind would check to see what was 'hidden' under the blotter.

That evening I re-measured the focal points. The pad had been moved. She'd been into the study.

I said nothing, but a few evenings later I had a joiner in to fit a lock on the study door. A good lock. A Chubb, with only two keys. Norah watched with blazing eyes and tightened lips. She knew I'd found her out.

Later, when we were all three at table, eating our evening meal, I opened the subject. Gently, of course. Jenny was present.

I dabbed my lips with my napkin and murmured, 'You may knock, Norah.'

'I beg your pardon?' She pretended not to understand.

'You may knock,' I repeated. 'If you wish to see me, when I'm in my study, you may knock. I'll always answer. But at all other times the door remains locked.'

There was a silence. I think she was struggling to keep control of herself. Jenny was there, remember.

Then at last she said, 'What if you're ill?'

'Am I likely to be ill?' I smiled.

Jenny looked worried, and said, 'Are you ill, Daddy?'

'No, my pet. Mummy tends to get a little melodramatic at times. That's all.'

'Things do happen,' insisted Norah. 'Sudden illnesses do happen.'

'It's a chance I'm prepared to take,' I said quietly.

The expression of complete non-understanding on Jenny's face troubled me. Then, she asked a terrible question.

'Why don't you love each other?'

Norah and I glanced at each other and I think, for a moment, something like compassion sparked between us. We'd tried so hard to hide our feelings for each other from our child, and we'd apparently failed.

I cleared my throat, then said, with as much mock-assurance as I could put into the words, 'That's a strange question to ask, my pet. Of course Mummy and I love each other. We're married, aren't we? We wouldn't be married if we didn't love each other.'

'We don't . . .' Norah stumbled on her words, then said, 'We're not demonstrative, darling. That's all.'

'That doesn't mean we don't love each other,' I added.

'I never see you kiss each other.'

'That doesn't mean we *don't*,' I smiled. 'Kissing isn't everything, my pet. It might be on television – at the cinema, perhaps – but that's only make-believe. In *real* life you don't have to be always kissing each other.'

It seemed to satisfy her. At least, in part. She may have thought she had strange parents. She may have seen the parents of one of her friends slobbering over each other. Who knows how a child of that age thinks?

That night, before she fell asleep, I visited her bedroom. I sat on the edge of the bed and tried to comfort her. Tried to reassure her.

'You see, my pet,' I explained, 'I'm tired. When I get home from work I'm tired. Sometimes very tired indeed. That makes me ill-tempered and not a very nice person to be with. Not always. But sometimes. But it wouldn't be fair to Mummy. To be grousing all the time. So, I go into my study, where I can only be cross with myself.'

'You sleep there,' she accused.

'I snore,' I lied. 'I snore very loudly, and Mummy's a very light sleeper. It keeps her awake.' I took the spare key from my pocket and slipped it under her pillow. 'Our secret,' I whispered. 'Just you and I. Nobody else. *You* don't have to knock. I'm never ill-tempered with you. Visit me. As often as you wish. Read with me. Listen to music with me. We'll make a world of our own. A secret, comfy world, where nobody can hurt us. *Our* world. Would you like that?'

She smiled and held out her arms.

As I hugged her goodnight, she whispered, 'Yes, Daddy. That would be lovely.'

Jenny was fifteen – closing on sixteen – when Norah's father retired. He'd been thrifty, invested wisely and he and his wife decided to retire to Dorset.

He'd been born in Dorset and, at a guess, he'd never really settled up north. I think some of his family lived in the Bere Regis area. For whatever reason, her parents decided to opt for a roses-round-the-door period for the rest of their lives and bought a place a few miles out of Frampton.

The thought of her parents moving so far away upset Norah far more than I might have imagined. Yet I

61

understood. I too had loved my parents. Nevertheless, her suggestion – a suggestion that almost amounted to a demand – came as a shock.

I was ending a chapter of a book, prior to retiring. As I recall, it was a rather drearily written travel book, and the knock on the study door came as a mild reprieve. I knew it wasn't Jenny – Jenny had already called in to say goodnight – and, truth to tell, I was a little surprised. Norah rarely visited the study. The slight humiliation of having to knock before gaining entrance was something she openly disliked.

However, I asked her in, she sat in the spare armchair, and I waited.

'I think *we* should move to Dorset,' she said, bluntly.

'In heaven's name, why?'

'You could sell the shop and set up again.'

'Where?' I steadied myself, and tried to remain calm.

'Frampton. Somewhere near Frampton.'

'Frampton?' I played for time.

'Somewhere near Frampton. Not too far from where Mother and Father are going to live.'

'You mean set up as a pharmacist?'

'Of course.'

'Just like that? Up sticks, and start somewhere else?'

'It's been done before.'

'Norah,' I said, heavily. 'Private pharmacists are going out of business left, right and sideways. The chain-store chemists are destroying them.'

'You're doing well enough.'

'We're *established*,' I pointed out. 'What I represent is three generations of reliability. I'm respected – like my father, like my grandfather – as a chemist who keeps a wide stock of drugs and medicines the chain-store people don't stock. I'm *known*.'

'You could sell. You could get a good price.'

'I could sell,' I agreed. 'I *might* be able to command a good price. But if I moved I'd be *unknown*. I'd have to start from scratch . . . and the odds would be very much in favour of failure.'

Her eyes shone, her lips hardened and then came the insults and counter-insults.

It was so stupid, but I suspect it happens to some degree in all marriages. This verbal sparring. This attempt to out-hurt each other. Equally, I suspect that in the majority of marriages it is accepted for what it is; a slight hiccup in an otherwise smooth-running relationship.

Indeed, it might even have been just that with us, had it not been that Norah meant to hurt. I knew her too well to have doubts. She'd visited the study to wound and, what is more, to wound without thought of mending whatever wound she might cause.

She snapped, 'I don't often ask for anything.'

'But when you do,' I countered, 'you ask for a lot.'

'You've no family to leave. You've no real friends in the town.'

'I have a daughter. *Our* daughter. Or is she of no importance?'

'I don't see what . . .'

'Her education will be interrupted.'

'We needn't go until she leaves school. After that . . .'

'*She* has friends.'

'I see.' The corners of her mouth twitched a little as the muscles tightened. 'We make ourselves miserable, for the sake of a teenage girl. Is that it?'

'We stay at Rogate-on-Sands.' I put finality in the words. '*I* certainly won't be miserable.'

'*I* will.'

'Nor will Jenny be miserable.'

'You can't speak for her.'

'She *might* be miserable if we leave. I'll not take that risk.'

'Herbert, she loves her grandparents.'

'That's not unusual.'

'You're suggesting she doesn't.'

'I'm suggesting nothing of the sort. I'm pointing out some very obvious facts. And one of them is that you are a remarkably selfish woman.'

'*I'm* selfish!'

'Good God, Norah, you *married* me.' It was one of the few times I've ever lost my temper. 'You were the one who made the vows. No registry office for you. The Big Occasion . . . if you recall. Bridesmaid, choirboys, the organ, the lot. *And* the old-fashioned ceremony. You'd do well to remember that. The vows you made. Something about "forsaking all others", wasn't it?'

'Of all the foul, mealy-mouthed . . .'

'I, on the other hand, made no solemn promise to traipse around the country in the wake of *your* parents. Nor did I agree to put our future in jeopardy at the whim of a stupid woman who forever has the urge to run home to "Mummy".'

'You really are a particularly disgusting man, aren't you?' she sneered.

'Am I expected to agree with that very biased assessment?'

'No! You aren't expected to agree with anything I say.'

'Good.' I raised the book back into a reading position. 'In that case, nobody is disappointed. Leave it at that. And, as a personal favour, let me read in peace.'

That argument was something of a watershed in our marriage. Nobody threw things. Neither of us struck the other. Nevertheless, it was the end of one more chapter.

Looking back, we might have grown together. Gradually – *very* gradually – the tension between us might have eased with age and, with the marriage of Jenny a few years later, we might have made a real effort at meeting somewhere midway.

But that supremely bitter argument killed even that remote possibility.

I never hated my wife. That I can say in all honesty. I think I am incapable of real hatred; the sort of hatred that devours all reason and becomes a canker of the soul. Equally, I suspect, I have never known the love one reads about in the great novels. The 'Brontë' brand of love. Something that develops into an emotion bigger than life itself.

In short, I am a moderate man. I find difficulty in being over-enthusiastic about anything. What few pleasures I enjoy are simple things. Inexpensive things. Pleasures that do not demand any form of obsession.

Therefore, I did not hate Norah.

I merely disliked her . . . intensely!

V

The detective chief inspector heeled the Interview Room door closed, then carried the tray to the table. He placed the tray midway between the man and where he (the detective chief inspector) was going to sit. The tray contained two beakers of steaming tea, a tin bowl of sugar, a carton of milk and a saucer on which were half a dozen digestive biscuits.

'Help yourself,' he murmured, as he lowered himself into the chair he'd vacated in order to bring the snack.

'I didn't expect this.' The man looked perplexed.

'We do things our way.' The detective chief inspector spooned sugar, then poured milk, into one of the beakers of tea. 'No rubber truncheons. No high-powered desk-lights. Is that what you had in mind?'

'No, but . . .' The man leaned forward slightly, and he sugared and milked the tea in the second beaker. He chewed his lower lip for a moment, then added, 'I didn't know *what* to expect.'

'Hit a man hard enough and often enough, and he'll say whatever you want him to say.' The detective chief inspector stirred the tea in his beaker. 'It won't necessarily be the truth, of course. Chances are it *won't* be.'

The man nodded, but still looked a little dazed.

The detective chief inspector bit into a biscuit and as he munched he murmured, 'No other women?'

'I've already said.'

'Not merely after you were married. *Before* you were married.'

'I've already said,' repeated the man, wearily. 'We were both virgins on our honeymoon.'

'Not the whole hog,' insisted the detective chief inspector. 'I mean the odd kiss and a cuddle behind the cycle shed. On the back row of some cinema.'

'No. Nothing.'

'No slap-and-tickle? No general horse-play, with the object of grabbing parts of a girl you were a little curious about?'

'Nothing,' repeated the man. He tasted the tea and reached for a biscuit. 'I've told you, Chief Inspector. I'm a very dull man. I was an equally dull youth.'

'And your wife? Norah?'

'I think I can say, with absolute certainty,' sighed the man, 'that she was equally – what's the expression? – "innocent".'

'Apart from your wife, then, the only people in your life – in your whole world – were your parents?'

'And Jenny. Jenny was more important than anybody.'

'Ah, yes. But Jenny came later.' The detective chief inspector waved what was left of the biscuit gently. 'I'm trying to figure things out, you see. You and your parents. Your wife and *her* parents. Almost identical bonds . . . wouldn't you say?'

'I suppose so.'

'And yet you didn't understand.'

'Understand?'

'When she so desperately wanted to move south with them.'

'It was impossible. I had the business to think about. I couldn't possibly have . . .'

67

'Ah, but you didn't *understand*.' The detective chief inspector popped what was left of the biscuit into his mouth. 'In her position – assuming your wife's parents had died, and *your* parents had decided to move to Dorset – wouldn't you have felt the same way? The same bond? The same urgent desire to move to within easy visiting distance?'

'I had the business to think about. Jenny to think about.'

'I'm not saying you would have gone. I'm suggesting you would have *felt* like going.'

'Perhaps.' It was a reluctant admission.

'Your daughter, your wife, your parents. A world of four people. *Your* world – the only world you had – surely there would have been a temptation. An attempt, perhaps. At the very least, a weighing-up of possible ways and means of keeping that world complete.'

'My world,' echoed the man, sadly.

'Precisely.'

'But Norah's world wasn't like that. In the beginning it might have been. But by that time she'd become tangled up with various women's groups.'

'Were they important to her?' The detective chief inspector sipped tea and reached for another biscuit. 'More important than her parents, perhaps?'

'Oh, no!' There was no hesitation. 'No. Not more important than her *parents*.'

'But a factor?'

'If so, I don't think they were an important factor.'

'Jenny?'

The man looked puzzled. As if he didn't understand the question.

'Was Jenny more important to your wife than her parents were?' amplified the detective chief inspector.

'I – er . . .' This time there was genuine hesitation, and the answer, when it came, was carefully worded. 'I think Norah loved Jenny. I'm sure she did. Of *course* she did. Not as much as *I* loved her, of course. But she certainly loved her.'

'More than she loved her parents?'

'I don't know.' The man shook his head slowly. 'I suppose so. I suppose she *must* have. After all, she was Jenny's mother. But she didn't show things. She kept her private feelings very much to herself.'

'Did she love *you*?' The detective chief inspector smiled as he asked the question, then bit into the biscuit.

'Norah?'

The detective chief inspector nodded.

'I – I don't know. I suppose so. In her own way, I suppose she did.'

'As much as you loved her?'

'That's hard to say.'

'More, perhaps?'

'I don't know. I *really* don't know.' There was a touch of desperation in the words.

'And yet,' said the detective chief inspector, 'there must have been *something*.'

'What?'

'At some time. After all, you married each other.'

'We drifted into it,' muttered the man.

'Come *on*, now.' Again the detective chief inspector smiled. It was a very knowledgeable smile. 'The two people you've been describing. The youth. The young man. The schoolgirl. The young woman. You and your wife, before the wedding. People like that don't "drift" into marriage. You weren't jet-types. You were staid. Unimaginative. Very slow to reach a decision. People like you don't "drift" into anything.'

'I suppose not.' The man sounded disconsolate. He repeated, 'I suppose not . . . really.'

'Jenny was no high-flying academic.' The detective chief inspector changed tack suddenly enough to make the man blink.

'I'm sorry. I don't . . .'

'No dullard.' The detective chief inspector munched as he

talked. 'Not thick – nothing like that . . . just that she wasn't university-fodder.'

'She wasn't a fool.' The man was suddenly on the defensive.

'Of course she wasn't.'

'If you're suggesting . . .'

'From what you've told me.' The detective chief inspector waved part of a biscuit. 'That's all. A normal, healthy kid, but no swot. She wasn't destined to pick up a hatful of Nobel Prizes. That's all I'm getting at.'

'She was as good as the rest.'

'Of course.'

'Better than most.'

'But not out front.'

'Not out front,' admitted the man, reluctantly.

'Therefore, going to Dorset – let's assume you'd agreed to move to where your parents-in-law were going – assuming that, it wouldn't *really* have interfered with anybody's schooling. Would it?'

'She was still at school.'

'Fifteen. Maybe sixteen. She wasn't going on to university . . . or was she?'

'No. Of course not.'

'Her schooldays were virtually at an end?'

'I suppose so.' The man paused, then began, 'In a manner of—'

'In a manner of *nothing*!' The interruption came in a hard and impatient tone. 'Dammit, man, she was on the point of leaving school.'

'Yes.' The man nodded.

'So-o . . .' The detective chief inspector resumed his previous friendly manner. 'It was a very empty excuse?'

'What?'

'That going to Dorset would – how did you put it? – "interrupt" her education. Her education had already ended.'

70

The man moved his head in bare acknowledgement.

'Therefore, an empty excuse?' pressed the detective chief inspector.

'What are you trying to prove?' Irritation edged the man's voice. 'All these questions? What, exactly, are you—'

'At the moment,' interrupted the detective chief inspector, mildly, 'I'm trying to prove nothing. Before I can *prove* anything – before I can even *believe* anything – I have to separate the truth from the wishful thinking.'

I think the argument about whether or not we followed her parents to Dorset upset Norah even more than it upset me. I can understand, of course. There was a bond which I had once had, but which I no longer had. Perhaps I forgot that bond.

Until after Jenny left school there was a steady, twice-weekly flow of letters. They were always addressed to Norah – never to 'Mr & Mrs' – and I saw no reason to open them, or even read them when they were left on the sideboard. Nor, come to that, did Norah discuss the contents of those letters.

I think I can be excused, therefore, for taking it for granted that they were the usual family correspondence and it was not until, on the face of things, Norah had settled down and accepted the situation that I was shocked into genuine concern.

And, at the same time, shocked into a show-down.

I arrived home one evening. The bungalow was empty, which in itself meant nothing. Jenny had her friends and Norah had the various and growing organisations of which she was becoming a part.

It was a fine day. Indeed, it had been a particularly sunny day and the evening promised to be warm and sultry. The last thing I needed was a heavy meal, therefore I opened the fridge and prepared myself a cheese salad.

The telephone rang as I was midway through the meal.

I remember thinking it must be one of Jenny's friends. Like most youngsters of her age, Jenny had become used to using the telephone for long and trivial conversations and, like most parents, I had tried to gently remind her that it was an expensive habit. I hadn't had much success.

I remember lifting the receiver with the firm intention of reminding whoever was calling that, even at the cheap rate, a thirty-minute conversation composed of empty verbiage seemed a little beyond the moderate use of a telephone.

I was surprised to hear Norah's voice.

'I hoped you'd be home by this time.'

The volume seemed poor. As if she wasn't making a local call . . . as, indeed, she was not.

I said, 'Yes?'

'I'm speaking from Mother's house.'

'Mother's house?' For the moment I could not quite comprehend.

'From Frampton,' she said, and her voice was quite calm. 'I have Jenny with me. We've been travelling all day.'

'What on earth are you doing down there? Is something wrong?'

'Wrong?' Now *she* couldn't understand.

'Is somebody ill? You should have . . .'

'Everybody is perfectly all right.'

'In that case, what are you . . . ?'

'I've left you, Herbert.'

'You've *what*?'

'Left you. I waited until Jenny had finished her schooling, then I made the appropriate arrangements.'

I recall I lowered the receiver from my face and took a few deep breaths to steady myself.

As I returned the receiver to my ear, Norah was saying '. . . and we arranged things by letter. But, of course, you weren't interested. You never even asked.'

'Norah!' I kept myself calm, spoke slowly and distinctly and made quite sure she understood exactly what I was saying. 'Norah, listen carefully. I will say this once. No more telephone conversations. No letters. Just this once, and be assured I mean every word.

'I have not turned you out of your home. You are free to return at any time you wish. At any time. But until you *do* return, there will be no money available. No cheques will be honoured. Tomorrow morning I will report that your bank card has been stolen. *And* your cheque book. There will be nothing. Nothing! I don't know what your father's financial position is, but I'll be surprised if he can afford to keep a wife, a daughter *and* a granddaughter. Other than a housewife, your own wage-earning capability is nil. You were trained for *nothing*. Not even the most menial office job. A cleaner, perhaps. A woman who goes out and "does" for better-off people. If your father is prepared to let you do that, you may *just* be able to repay him for what it costs to keep you. Perhaps even a little towards the cost of keeping Jenny.

'As far as *I* am concerned, I will not make this situation known, unless I am asked. But if I *am* asked, I'll tell the truth. That you've left me, and taken Jenny. I will volunteer no possible reason. I don't *know* of a reason. They may make of it what they please. What rumours your friends will see fit to invent is something you can guess better than I. But, rest assured, I shall neither deny nor verify those rumours.

'This much, however, I promise you. If you go to a solicitor – if you go *near* a solicitor – if I receive a single communication from a solicitor's office – this remarkably droll situation will end up in court. You will be made to justify this ridiculous action. You will be made to say exactly *why* – and for no good reason – you have seen fit to leave a very good home, sacrifice a particularly handsome house-keeping allowance and take our child half the length of England in order to be near your parents.

'You have your reasons, I presume. I hope they are good reasons. But whatever those reasons, I'm sure they'll make interesting reading in the local newspapers.'

I lowered the receiver onto its rest as she started to answer. I had no wish to hear whatever silly and empty excuses she had to offer.

The ultimatum had been given. The choice now rested with her.

It took her almost two weeks to come to her senses. I'd had one letter, but I hadn't even opened it, much less read it. Still sealed, I'd torn it to shreds and thrown it into the waste-paper basket.

Then, one dreary day – one of those will-it-rain-won't-it-rain sort of days – complete capitulation occurred. I remember having watched the visitors walking along the promenade, looking both uncertain and unhappy. If the sun came out, they wanted to enjoy it. If, on the other hand, the threatened rain came it might be a good idea to make use of the matinée at the local three-screen cinema, pending a better evening.

We (the shopkeepers) can read these signs, and feel sorry for the holidaymakers. We even feel vaguely ashamed that Rogate-on-Sands is spoiling hard-earned leisure by being deliberately fickle.

I know it wasn't far from closing time when Jenny almost ran into the shop. The assistant called a greeting but other than a passing smile Jenny hurried into the dispensary.

'Daddy, we're home!'

She held out her arms and we hugged before I bent to kiss her forehead.

Not knowing how much *she* knew, I contented myself with, 'I've missed you, pet. I've missed you a lot.'

'It was a lovely holiday, though.'

'Good.' My mind raced, in an attempt to work out what she'd been told.

'Grandad took us all to Weymouth one day. Then another day he took us all to Lyme Regis.'

'You had a good time?' I smiled.

'A *lovely* time.' Then, hurriedly, 'But it would have been even better if you'd been able to come.'

'Work, my pet.' I settled a hand on her shoulder, then asked, 'Is Mummy OK? Has the holiday done *her* good?'

'She's had headaches. Lots of bad headaches.'

'Oh, dear.'

'But I think she's better now. She sent me to tell you we'd arrived home, and that you mustn't go to some café. She'll have dinner ready for you when you arrive home.'

* * *

75

I remain amazed at the way in which Norah dismissed what could have been the wrecking of our marriage. More than that, what could have been a lasting traumatic experience for our child.

And yet . . .

Outwardly, she was calm. Almost friendly. But inside she must have been seething. Common sense insists that she must have recognised and accepted complete defeat, and realised that I'd forced her to crawl back to where she belonged, without allowing her to retain a vestige of pride.

I didn't crow. I matched her, calmness for calmness. But she must have *known*. This, despite the easy lie that she'd 'been on a short holiday' at her parents' home, which is what she told her friends.

Yet, oddly, that is the lie she enacted, and to me, that first evening.

The day had righted itself and the lowering sun had warmed the whole world. It was dusk, with a blue-grey sky overhead with crimson to the west, then darkening into purple shading into early night to the east. The walled rear-garden of the bungalow seemed the most private place on earth. Above the seven-foot-high surround yellow street lights were on, and already casting squat shadows of the trees upon the grass of the lawn. Jenny was in her room, earphones cutting her off from reality, as she listened to the latest cacophonic howlings of some soon-to-be-forgotten pop group.

Norah and I strolled and talked. Never louder than was necessary to carry the words the short distance between us. We said things, but meant other things, but we both knew the other was perfectly aware of what was hidden behind the screen of words.

'It was a nice break,' she said. 'A nice holiday.'

'Is that what it was?'

'That's what it *ended* as.'

'A short holiday with Jenny,' I murmured.

'I had to see how things worked out.'

'Naturally.'

'I had to decide.'

'I'm delighted you reached the right decision.'

'Did anybody ask?' There was, perhaps, a slight tremble in her voice.

'About what?'

'About me being away.'

'You were on holiday . . . weren't you?'

'I mean did anybody . . . ?'

'I kept myself to myself . . . as usual.'

'So nobody knows?'

'Jenny's been on holiday. You've been with her.'

'It seemed wise to put it that way. Pending whatever decision I reached.'

'And now you've reached a decision,' I said, gently.

'I'm back, aren't I?'

'It could be a flying visit, of course. To "collect" things.'

'No. It's not that.'

'You'll have discussed things with your parents.'

'Yes. In a way.'

'How big a way?'

'I discussed things. Fairly thoroughly.'

'And?'

'They don't want to see you again.'

'Unless they come north, that can be arranged without difficulty.'

'They won't be coming north.'

'But you *are* back?' If the question had a certain teasing quality, who can blame me?

'I'm here, with you, aren't I?'

'It won't happen again.'

She thought it was a question, and said, 'I doubt it.'

'It *won't* happen again,' I repeated quietly. 'The next time, don't waste money on a return ticket. Your key won't fit the lock when you get back.'

'There won't be a "next time".' There wasn't much expression in the words, but they added up to unconditional surrender. She added, 'My options are very limited . . . in view of Jenny.'

'Hadn't you realised that?'

'Don't turn her against me.' There was an unusual pleading quality in the remark.

'Have I ever?'

'She may need me, one day.'

'She needs both of us. All the time. That's something else you'd do well to realise.'

Life changed. It had to. Norah had made too big a fool of herself for things to continue as before.

That first meal on her return home was one of the last meals we shared. Thereafter, she ate before I returned and left me food, more or less prepared, while she joined her female friends at their various junketings. I think she joined just about every 'organisation' in Rogate-on-Sands. The various societies. The countless 'do-good' groups. There wasn't a flag day, there wasn't a sponsored event that she wasn't a part of. Usually on the administrative side. I suppose it kept her busy – stopped her mind from dwelling upon the utter stupidity of her jaunt to Dorset – and it kept us apart. Which, presumably, was the main object.

More than ever, we lived separate lives. We shared the same home, the same roof and walls, the same garden. To outsiders (and, hopefully, to Jenny) we were an average, staid, unexciting married couple. Odd, perhaps, that we so rarely spoke to, or even at, each other . . . and nobody seemed to notice.

Not for us the walking-hand-in-hand sign of marital conviviality. On the few occasions we went out together we walked side-by-side, but never touched. In the car, Jenny sat in front with me, while Norah had the rear seat to herself.

I recall when Jenny was eighteen – at the birthday treat I

gave for her at The Beaconfield – we sat at a table in the very sumptuous dining room. It was a table for four, with the empty chair between Norah and myself. I helped Jenny through the menu, then ordered for the two of us. Norah gave her own order.

The waiter looked puzzled, then asked, 'Are you all in the same party, sir?'

'Give the bill to me,' I smiled.

It answered his question, but it was an answer which left my wife in little doubt as to *her* position.

For the first few months after the Dorset interlude, I worried a little.

Of necessity, I'd had to make arrangements with the bank for Norah to be issued with a new bank card, and that meant she could draw as much money as she wished, pending the state of our joint account. She could, had she so wished, have hit me hard in the pocket, but she didn't. Perhaps she *daren't.* To be on the safe side, I opened a second account, in my own name, moved money and made sure that the joint account remained very modest.

I wasn't mean, or pinch-penny. I met the household bills and renewed what I considered (and still consider) a handsome housekeeping allowance.

Nor did Jenny go short of anything.

VI

The detective chief inspector pressed the light switch and the strip-lighting hissed and flickered for a moment before flooding the Interview Room with bluish-white light. It seemed a very appropriate light, in that it cast few shadows. Like the Interview Room – like the man conducting the interview – it had no time for dark corners.

The detective chief inspector returned to his chair, then asked, 'What was in the study?'

'I've already told you. A desk. A couple of chairs . . .'

'What was it you didn't want your wife to see?'

'Nothing.' The man's eyes widened in amazement. 'I've already explained. Just privacy. That's all I sought.'

'A bolt?' suggested the detective chief inspector, mildly. 'They come far cheaper than Chubb locks.'

'When I wasn't there, you see,' explained the man. 'When I was at the shop. I didn't want her nosing around.'

'So, it was rather *more* than privacy?'

'What?'

'When you weren't there – when you were at work – privacy didn't come into it. You weren't *in* the study. No privacy to interfere with . . . surely?'

'She was – she was looking at my things.'

'What things?'

'My papers, my books, my stamp collection. Everything.'

'You didn't even want her to *look*?' The detective chief inspector raised an eyebrow.

'I'm – I'm a very private man. I'm sorry if that sounds peculiar, but . . .'

'You were also a *married* man.'

'Yes.' The man nodded, as he tried to follow the detective chief inspector's line of conversation.

'Share and share alike . . . all that sort of thing.'

'We'd little in common.'

'On the contrary.' The detective chief inspector smiled. 'You were very much *like* each other.'

'You – you didn't even know her.' The man stared.

'According to your father.'

'What?'

'Before you married . . . remember? The suggestion that you were too much like each other. You agreed . . . didn't you?'

The man frowned.

'Didn't you?' pressed the detective chief inspector.

'In some ways.' It was a reluctant admission.

The detective chief inspector took the packet of cigarettes from his pocket. He opened it and this time offered the packet to the man.

'I don't smoke,' said the man.

'I do.' The detective chief inspector placed a cigarette between his lips. 'I claim the right to kill myself.'

'And others? Those who don't smoke, but are obliged to breathe your cigarette smoke, second-hand?'

'And *that*, from a poisoner?' The detective chief inspector touched the flame of a match to the cigarette. He continued, 'Let's talk about music. You like music?'

'I've already told you.'

'What you would call "good" music?'

81

'Classical music. *Real* music.'

'But not your wife?'

'I don't doubt that she would have called it "music". The candy-floss tunes played at the pier pavilion.'

'Not Mozart, for example?'

The man smiled a condescending smile, and that was answer enough.

'And yet,' said the detective chief inspector, gently, 'you refused to listen to a Mozart symphony.'

'When?' The impression was that having asked the quick question the man's mind flipped back a few years, and he added, 'Oh, you mean Mozart's "Prague"?'

'You were reading Hardy at the time,' said the detective chief inspector, gently.

'It was television,' muttered the man.

'It was an olive branch. You even recognised it as such, and you rejected it.'

'I do not like watching a televised symphony concert. The man responsible for the cameras never credits the viewer with—'

'You don't like strolling along the promenade.'

'I see the promenade enough, while I'm at—'

'All you wanted to do was sit in that study, read, listen to the music *you* wanted to hear, without even the inconvenience of being polite.' The detective chief inspector drew deeply on the cigarette, then let the smoke trickle from his nostrils before he continued, 'You wanted both the cherry and the cake, my friend. Every time. Life on your terms . . . or not at all.'

'You think that's why I poisoned her?' The man looked strangely disappointed.

'According to you, rather than the stigma of divorce.'

'Had she been given a choice—'

'*Was* she given a choice?' snapped the detective chief inspector.

'If you mean, did I *ask* her . . . ?'

'You could have divorced her, when she went to Dorset. She must have known *that*.'

'I suppose so.'

'She apparently chose the "stigma", then.'

'I made a choice,' sighed the man.

'For *her*?'

'It was the choice I thought she'd have made.'

'*If* you poisoned her.'

'You think I *didn't*? You *still* think I didn't?'

'I'm beginning to wonder,' said the detective chief inspector. 'Am I talking to a murderer? Or a madman? A self-satisfied prat? Or a psychiatrist's museum-piece? Or maybe just a kinky bastard who for some twisted reason wants to waste my time?'

'You don't believe *that*, Chief Inspector,' said the man, mildly.

'No.' The detective chief inspector's voice was heavy with disgust. '*That* I no longer believe. Earlier, perhaps, but not now. There's too much detail. Detail that can be checked. Detail that's already *being* checked . . . for your information.'

The man smiled, and said, 'I rather thought when you left me it wasn't *only* to bring tea and biscuits.'

'You've no objection?' Then, hurriedly, 'Not that it matters a damn whether you object or not.'

The man shrugged gentle resignation.

'What about Jenny?' growled the detective chief inspector.

'Jenny?'

'Your daughter. She'll have to be told. Next of kin, and all that.'

'She'll be upset.'

'Upset? Not shocked?'

'Shocked, if you like.'

'Make a choice.' The detective chief inspector didn't even try to disguise his growing impatience. 'Make *another* choice. "Upset" or "shocked"?'

'That,' murmured the man, 'would be splitting hairs.'

'Fine.' The detective chief inspector took a last inhalation from the cigarette, then screwed it into shreds in the ashtray. He repeated, 'Fine, let's split a few hairs. We've all night ahead of us.'

Norah tried to argue me into allowing Jenny to go out to work. In fairness, I think she did it for what she thought were the best of reasons, but she was wrong. Jenny – *my* Jenny -- was going to take orders from nobody!

Jenny was going to assist her mother about the house and garden. Perhaps work behind the shop counter when an assistant was either ill or on holiday. But that was going to be the absolute limit . . . and only that if Jenny agreed.

Norah had other ideas.

Jenny had left school less than a month before. I was eating a moderately well-prepared evening meal while Norah was moving about the kitchen doing her chores, when she opened the subject in her usual brusque manner.

'What sort of job do you think Jenny should try for?'

I remember I was eating a fish-and-cheese dish. Something Norah had, perhaps, picked up from one of the women's magazines. Or, perhaps, at one of the 'talks' given to the various female groups of which she was now a part. I know it was rather tasty and different from the normal run of meals.

I hedged a little by asking, 'Has she mentioned the subject?'

'No.'

'Then why should you?'

Without looking round from the sink she said, 'She's young, and she's healthy.'

'That's no answer.'

'I think she should go out to work.'

'Earn her living?' I mocked, gently.

'That's what it boils down to.'

'I can afford to keep my own daughter,' I assured her.

'That isn't the point, Herbert.'

'We certainly don't need the pittance she'll be able to earn.'

'Nor is *that* the point.'

'Is she complaining?' I asked.

'No.' She stacked crockery into the dishwasher. 'But I

85

think she'd benefit. A course at a secretarial college, perhaps.'

'A waste of time, and a waste of money. She's not going to be a secretary.'

'Or there's a vacancy going at Marks and Spencer's.'

'You know that, do you?'

'I know the wife of the manager. The job's Jenny's, if she wants it.'

'And *does* she want it?'

'I haven't asked her. I thought I'd have a word with you first.'

'My daughter is not going to work in a chain store.'

'They're very choosey.'

'I'm not suggesting she's not good enough,' I snapped. 'I'm saying she's *too* good.'

'Don't be ridiculous!'

'My daughter, a shop-girl?' I was angry, and made no pretence. 'Good God, woman! Where's your pride?'

'I haven't much pride left.' She spoke in a tight, but very controlled voice. 'But I'm prepared to sacrifice what I *have* got to give my daughter a chance in life.'

'Being a shop-girl?' I sneered.

'Herbert, it's far more than that.' She turned and leaned against the sink edge. 'She needs some degree of independence.'

'Independence?'

'Part-independence,' she corrected herself.

'What she earns – whatever she earns – won't pay for her clothes. Won't pay for her hobbies.'

'That's not important.'

'She works for *nothing*?' I mocked. 'She works for the *fun* of it? She trudges through the town in all weathers, in order to give her "character"? Is that the silly argument you're putting forward?'

'You've spoiled her,' she said, heavily.

'She's my daughter,' I said, harshly. 'While I'm alive she doesn't have to work for a living. I owe her that, and I'll give

86

her that. All I ask is that you teach her to be a competent housewife.'

'Like me?' There was a depth of bitterness in the question.

'Your housekeeping – your cooking – you have yet to hear me complain. Teach her those things. I'll teach her the rest.'

She was my daughter. All other people were unimportant by comparison. Norah was unimportant. Even *I* was unimportant. The only thing that mattered was that Jenny should have a happy and uninterrupted span of teenage years.

She played tennis, she swam and she had parties. In the winter she went to dances, skated on the park pond or, muffled in woollies, sat around driftwood bonfires on the beach and, to guitar accompaniment, sang mild and sad songs of protest with her friends. She didn't have to work, she was far too busy *living*, and that was as it should be.

Sometimes – not often, but *sometimes* – I left my study and wandered to where I knew she'd be. To stand in the shadows and, without her knowing I was there, to watch. Not to spy. I'd taught her too well for her to need spying upon. Merely to see, and verify. To make sure that I had, indeed, created a superbly happy youngster. A creature of laughter, without fear and without inhibition.

And when we were together, alone and comfortable in the study, we had no secrets. She asked questions, and I answered them. Anything and everything. Or we listened to music, or we read, or, as sometimes happened, we argued a little. But without bitterness. With mutual love. And, in some strange way, the arguments seemed to draw us even closer.

Three wonderful years. Idyllic years, as far as Jenny was concerned. I'm sure they were. I rarely saw her without a smile on her face.

Those never-to-be-forgotten years. They were worth everything. They were reason enough for my living.

Then, less than two weeks after her nineteenth birthday, Jenny was kidnapped.

87

INTERLUDE WITH JENNY

VII

The detective chief inspector said, 'Y'see, Jenny . . .' He smiled, then added, 'I may call you Jenny, mayn't I?'

'Of course.'

'I'm here for a reason,' explained the detective chief inspector. 'It's a reason I can't explain – not for the moment – other than that it involves your father, and a certain story he's seen fit to tell me.'

'A story?' The young woman looked puzzled.

'A complaint . . . of a sort.'

'What about?'

'Later, maybe. We have certain confidences to respect. Suffice to say it involves you having been kidnapped some years ago.'

'Oh!'

'That's just *part* of the story.'

She chewed her bottom lip for a moment, then ventured, 'It's a thing I don't like talking about. We've tried to forget it. To pretend it didn't happen. It was a sort of mutual agreement. We deliberately decided – we-ell, perhaps not *deliberately* – but we *seemed* to decide. Mother, Father and I. We never mentioned it.'

'When did it happen?' pressed the detective chief inspector.

'It was just after my nineteenth birthday. About a week after. Possibly little more than a week.' She seemed to have difficulty in marshalling her thoughts. 'There was this party. It was a party given by a friend of an acquaintance. A sort of "open" party. Anybody and everybody was invited.'

The detective chief inspector nodded his understanding and smiled encouragement.

She continued, 'A group of us decided to go. To more or less crash it. The party, I mean. It – it was a mistake. I didn't know anybody when we got there. Nobody! And I didn't *really* enjoy it. It was too noisy, with much too much to drink. Far too wild a party for my taste.'

'You don't mind me calling to see you at this hour?' murmured the detective chief inspector, apologetically.

'No. Not at all. It's just that . . .'

'Good.' The accompanying grin had a paternal quality. 'You were saying . . . the party?'

'It wasn't a very nice party.' She wrinkled her nose at the memory. 'Everybody seemed to be drinking silly cocktails. And smoking. Everybody was smoking cigarettes. In those days, non-smokers were the minority but at that party *everybody* was smoking. I rather suspect some of the "cigarettes" were reefers. That's what we called them in those days. Reefers. Marijuana, smoked like a cigarette. But the smell's quite different from the smell of cigarette tobacco.'

'I know,' agreed the detective chief inspector.

'It's not . . .' Suddenly, she looked startled.

'What?'

'Father. It hasn't to do with dope, has it?'

'Dope?'

'Drugs. Illegal drugs. Him being a chemist. Surely he hasn't . . .'

'It has nothing to do with illegal drugs,' the detective chief inspector assured her.

'You'd tell me? You'd tell me, if it was *that*?'

'I'd tell you,' said the detective chief inspector, solemnly. Then, 'Let's get back to the party.'

'It was . . .' She moistened her lips, then continued, 'It was about ten o'clock. I suddenly felt ill. Very ill. Wobbly. Dizzy. It wasn't drink. I think I'd had about two of those cocktail things. I wasn't drunk. I was ill. And this man . . .'

'Which man?'

'Just – just a man. I didn't know him. I haven't met him since. I know he was older than me. Quite a few years older. He must have spotted that I looked rather terrible, and he came up to me.'

'*He* approached *you*?'

'Oh, yes. He said something like, "Lassie, you look like death." As I recall, those were his exact words. "Lassie, you look like death."'

'And?'

'I think I nodded my agreement. I – I don't think I spoke a word to him throughout the entire incident. I felt ill. I trusted him. He looked a decent chap, he had a pleasant voice and a nice smile. I had no reason *not* to trust him. I know the atmosphere in the room was foul and when he suggested a breath of fresh air it seemed a good idea.'

For a moment she sat silent and pensive. Almost sad. As if catching memories of things she had long tried to forget.

The detective chief inspector waited.

Then she continued: 'It seemed a good idea. To let him guide me through the French windows and out onto the lawn. It had lots of fairy lights and the whole garden was patches of different colours and shadows. There was an extension loud-speaker from the record player, and some of them were dancing on the grass. There was a lot of kissing and a lot of snogging in the shadows. It was that sort of a party. Not an orgy. I'm not saying that. But, at a guess, there was some heavy groping going on. It was wild . . . but not *too* wild.'

93

'The sort of party you were used to?' suggested the detective chief inspector, gently.

'Oh, Lord, no.' The wisp of a smile touched her lips. 'I wouldn't have gone, had I known.'

'The – er – the man,' murmured the detective chief inspector.

'I beg your pardon?'

'What happened next?'

'Oh, that.' She paused, then said, 'He took me to a seat in the shadows. Away from the crowd and the noise. He didn't try anything. I don't think he even touched me. Not even on the arm, as he led the way.'

A hint of disbelief touched the detective chief inspector's expression.

'It's true,' she insisted. 'He seemed very worried. That's all. Rather paternal, in a nice sort of way.'

The detective chief inspector nodded, slowly, and seemed to accept the assurance.

'He sat down beside me on the bench,' she said, 'and asked me if I felt better. I don't even remember answering him. That's when I fainted . . . or something. After that, I don't remember *anything*.'

'You fainted?' murmured the detective chief inspector.

'I – y'know – passed out.'

'A complete blank?'

'Until I woke up in what I think was the ward of some hospital. One of those tiny, one-bed wards.'

'Nothing?' The detective chief inspector narrowed his eyes slightly.

'I beg your pardon?'

'You remember *nothing*?'

'No . . . nothing.'

'You can't remember being manhandled? Anything like that?'

'Oh, no. I was treated well enough. I wasn't knocked about. Nobody tried to rape me. Nobody swore at me.

Nothing like that. In fact, when I discovered I *had* been kidnapped, I could hardly believe it. It wasn't *like* being kidnapped.'

'I've never *been* kidnapped,' smiled the detective chief inspector.

'I'm sorry. I don't . . .'

'I wouldn't know *what* it feels like.'

'No. Of course not.' She returned the smile. 'All I know is that I awakened in this bed, with a nurse alongside me.'

'Can you describe the nurse?'

'It's – it's a long time since it . . .'

'Try,' encouraged the detective chief inspector.

'At a guess . . .' Jenny frowned her concentration. 'At a guess she was about as old as Mother, but thinner. Much more severe. I'd even call her gaunt. But she wasn't frightening at all. She was very grim-looking and she wore steel-rimmed spectacles. I think that made her look even sterner than she was. She was very slim and very straight-backed and she had long, bony fingers.'

'Just her?' said the detective chief inspector.

'What?'

'Just the one nurse?'

'Oh, no. There were others. But she was the main nurse. Two others looked after me, at various times, but the one I first saw seemed to be in charge.'

'They never left you?'

'No. I was never left alone. There was a comfortable armchair in one corner of the room, and one of the nurses was always with me.'

'You stayed in bed?'

'Oh, yes. I never left the bed, other than to visit the toilet or the bathroom, and they were through a door leading directly from the bedroom.'

'And the door was always kept open?'

'Of course.'

'Of course.' The detective chief inspector nodded, sagely.

Then he asked, 'How did you feel? When you'd come round, I mean. Did you feel ill? A headache, perhaps?'

'Oh, yes, I was ill. It wasn't a natural illness – I know that *now* – but I was certainly ill. Something brought on and prolonged by the capsules they gave me. Some sort of drug, I suppose.'

'But you *were* ill?' pressed the detective chief inspector.

'Oh, yes.'

'What did you think was wrong with you?'

'I didn't know. It never entered my head to ask. I'd always been so healthy. This was the first real "illness" I'd ever had, and I truly believed I *was* ill.' She paused, then continued, 'I was never fully awake, you see. Never strong enough to even think without conscious effort.'

'What about food?'

'As I recall, I ate well enough. Nothing too heavy, of course. Typical "hospital" food. But, you see, I wasn't *physically* sick. I think it's true to say I wasn't physically *ill*. It was a mental thing, really.'

'You knew you'd been kidnapped, of course?'

'It's – it's hard to say.' She seemed to seek for words. 'I knew eventually of course. But at the time . . .'

Again, she seemed to have difficulty in making herself understood. The detective chief inspector waited, but she seemed unable to continue.

'What about visitors?' he asked. 'If you didn't know you'd been kidnapped – if you thought you were ill – didn't you find it strange that even your parents didn't come to see you?'

'I – er – I think I asked for Mother a couple of times. In fact, I'm sure I did. But nobody gave me a straightforward answer. When I was lucid – on the few occasions when I *was* lucid – I tended to wonder where she was, and why she didn't visit me, but I seemed to be in good hands and I comforted myself with the thought that there must be a reason for her not seeing me.' Then, almost apologetically, 'To tell the

96

truth, it didn't seem to matter too much.'

'Concentrate on the lucid moments,' said the detective chief inspector.

She nodded and waited.

'Didn't you *ever* wonder where you were? Weren't you ever *curious*?'

'Of course. I recall . . .' She cupped her jaw in the palm of one hand and her eyes went a little out of focus. 'I recall looking through a window. Just once. I was still in bed, but the haziness had worn off a little. The nurse was in the room, as usual, but she had her back to me and I had a clear view through the top panes of the window.

'I don't think we were on the ground floor. The first floor, perhaps. No higher than the second floor. That's the impression I had. The lower panes of the window were ribbed, so nobody could see through them, but the upper panes were clear. And I saw mountains in the distance.'

'Mountains?' The detective chief inspector leaned a little further forward in his chair.

'*Real* mountains.' She re-focused her eyes. 'Snow-covered peaks. Not the sort of thing you get in the Lake District. Or Scotland or in Snowdonia. The sort of mountains I'd only seen on postcards or on television travel documentaries.'

'Didn't you wonder?' The detective chief inspector's tone held a degree of incredulity. 'Weren't you curious about where you might be?'

'I've explained.' And now there was a hint of petulance in her voice. 'I didn't *know* I'd been kidnapped. Not at the time.'

'Quite.' The detective chief inspector nodded mild and soothing understanding. 'But the view from the window?'

'As I've said. Mountains. Mountains with snow on their peaks.'

'On the Continent, somewhere?'

'Of course. When I knew what had . . .'

'No!' The detective chief inspector raised a hand from his

knee. 'Before you actually *knew*. When you saw the mountains through the window. Did you realise you were on the Continent?'

'It – it seemed likely.' She frowned. 'Ye-es, I suppose I did. If I was capable of thinking *anything*.'

'The nurses?' pressed the detective chief inspector. 'They spoke to you, of course. They said things.'

'Yes.'

'And their accents?'

'They all three spoke very good English.'

'By that, you mean they were foreigners?'

'I . . .' She hesitated. Her face creased into an expression of concentration. Then she said, 'I suppose so.'

'The Alps?' suggested the detective chief inspector.

'I beg your pardon?'

'The mountains you saw from the window. The Alps?'

'They could have been,' she agreed.

'The French Alps? The Swiss Alps? The Austrian Alps?'

'I – I really don't know.'

'From the accent of the nurses?' explained the detective chief inspector. 'A French accent, perhaps?'

'No, not French. Guttural, I think. Guttural, if anything.'

'Austrian,' smiled the detective chief inspector. 'Let's settle for Austrian . . . provisionally. Somewhere in Austria. Within sight of the Alps.'

'Does that help?' She seemed anxious.

'Not a great deal,' admitted the detective chief inspector. He grinned, then added, 'It eliminates China.'

'No . . . I mean Father. Does it help *him*?'

'It might.' The detective chief inspector rose to his feet. 'It won't do him any harm.'

'He's in trouble, isn't he?' she sighed.

'I don't yet know.' The detective chief inspector smiled, paternally. 'Go back to bed, Jenny. Don't worry about things. *If* he's in trouble, you'll be the first to know.'

* * *

98

I should have told the police about the kidnapping. That goes without saying. The police are the professionals. The experts. They know how to handle these situations. One *should* tell the police at such times.

But I wonder how many *don't*? How much money is paid out, in secret? How many men are like me? How many men are afraid of what might happen if they *do* tell the police?

Jenny's life was at stake. The price was a paltry ten thousand. That's all. Ten thousand pounds! I wasn't going to risk her life for *that* amount.

The phone call came before we'd even missed Jenny. She was at a party somewhere. That's what *we* thought. Norah took the call, then came to tell me somebody wanted to speak to me, personally. Later, she said it was from a kiosk. When we realized what had happened, and we talked things over, she said she'd heard the bleeps before the coin was inserted.

Something was being held over the mouthpiece. A handkerchief, I suspect. But *something*. It was a man's voice, but it was muffled.

He said, 'Don't even think of going to the police, otherwise you won't see your daughter alive again.'

He started with that warning. I tried to ask questions, but he wouldn't listen.

He said, 'We have your daughter. She'll be returned, unharmed, if you follow instructions. Get ten thousand pounds in used tens and fives. Get the money from the bank. Have it ready. I'll contact you within the next forty-eight hours.'

Then he rang off.

At first we didn't understand. We didn't even *believe*. But we rang round Jenny's friends and they couldn't help. She'd gone with them to this party, but they'd missed her when it was time to leave. That's all they could tell us. They thought she'd left on her own. Perhaps with somebody she'd met, but they hadn't seen her with anybody in particular.

That was when we really accepted the fact that the telephone call might be genuine, and not some nasty-minded hoax. It was a gradual thing, and it became real – acceptable – as we sat up all that night.

By morning we were both in a bad state, but we both realised we had to act as normally as possible. We daren't go to the police. We daren't even report her missing.

The next two days were quite terrible. Terrible beyond description. It was – how can I put it? – a little like being a good swimmer, but being in mid-Atlantic. You could live, and you had to live, but you didn't *want* to live because things seemed so absolutely hopeless. Whatever you did and however you tried, it was going to be impossible to *achieve* anything without help.

I withdrew the money from the bank. In tens and fives, as the man had said. I counted it out into five-hundred-pound bundles, then locked it away in my desk which, in turn, was locked away in my study. I didn't want to go to the shop, but we agreed that I *had* to, in order not to attract any attention. But Norah stayed by the phone all day. At night, we even slept in shifts. One of us by the telephone, sitting in an armchair, in case it rang.

With hindsight, I must have been under some sort of surveillance. I must have been because the call, when it came, wasn't to either the bungalow or the shop.

It was at lunchtime, on the second day. I'd left the shop for a quick snack at a local public house. I recall I was forcing myself to eat a cheese salad when the landlord called me to one end of the bar and handed me the telephone receiver.

It was the same terse voice. The same muffled tone, and very specific instructions.

'Your wife brings the money. She comes alone. She carries the money in a tartan holdall, with a zipped top. She comes by road. She drives to Dover and catches the evening ferry to Calais. She keeps the holdall on the front passenger's seat, alongside her. Do things right, and you'll see your daughter again.'

I did exactly as instructed. I hunted around the shops and bought a tartan, zip-topped holdall. I packed the money into it, then, with a small overnight bag for her personal things, Norah set off for Dover that same evening.

Those next two days!

I learned hatred in those few hours. I almost learned madness. I don't know how many times, but on at least four occasions, I was on the point of contacting the police. I had *nobody*. Not even Norah.

That first day – the day after Norah had left – I went to the shop and tried to work. It was impossible. I was unable to concentrate. I couldn't trust myself to measure the prescriptions. At midday I decided to close the pharmacy and go home until I knew something.

Thereafter, I spent most of the time pacing the rooms of the bungalow and drinking black coffee.

I am a tidy man. A neat man. I have even been accused of being fastidious. But for two days I neither washed nor shaved. I hadn't even the wit to change my clothes; to wear something more comfortable than shoes and waistcoat. Such was my state of mind.

Norah telephoned on the third day.

She'd paid the money, and was telephoning from some hotel in Switzerland. I asked the obvious question.

'Is Jenny with you?'

'Yes.'

'Let me speak to her.'

'She's in her room, recovering.'

'Recovering?'

'I can see the improvement, almost by the hour.'

'What have they *done* to her?'

'Drugged her.'

'Oh my God!'

'She's been drugged for most of the time.'

'For heaven's sake, get her home.'

'Don't be silly, Herbert. She's through it now.'

'*Get her home.*'

'She's not yet fit to travel.'

'By air. Come back by air. Let's get her into hospital.'

'Don't be ridiculous. She can't travel alone.'

'You'll be with her. What on earth are you . . .'

'I have the car. Remember?'

'Oh!'

'Less than a week, I think. Then she'll be fit enough. I'll telephone each day.'

In fact, they were away for a full week. Norah telephoned every evening and, each time, insisted that Jenny was improving, but slowly. Nevertheless, it was comforting and I gradually regained my composure and was back at work before they returned.

Jenny looked a different person when she arrived home. She'd been so lively. So happy and filled with the joy of living. Now she was pale and lack-lustre. She hardly ever smiled, spoke only when she was spoken to and spent much of her time alone, in her room.

Norah took her to our local medic, but the truth is she never regained that happy-go-lucky attitude to life she had once had. Something died while she was in Switzerland (or wherever it was they kept her) and, hard as I tried, I could never bring it back to life.

Norah would never tell me the details of her trip to Europe to collect Jenny. Merely that a man had approached her on the Calais ferry, had taken over the car and had driven – virtually non-stop – to somewhere near Gargellen. He'd checked the money before meeting up with an ambulance, then Jenny had been carried, unconscious, from the ambulance and placed in the car.

That, it seems, was the last Norah saw of them.

They weren't far from the Swiss border and, when Jenny had come round, Norah drove to a small hotel near Weesen and booked in. It was from there that she telephoned me.

Beyond that bare information she refused to go. I had the impression that she'd been warned to say as little as possible. I rather think she was frightened. What could happen once could happen again.

I respected her decision.

Jenny was back, and that was the main thing.

Then, of course, a year or so later, Jenny met Walter. They began seeing each other regularly. Eventually they married.

THE INTERVIEW
CONTINUED

VIII

'Kidnapping?' The detective chief inspector sucked his teeth, meditatively. 'Not a very clever thing to do. Not to tell the police, I mean.'

'Do you have a child?' asked the man.

'No.'

'In that case, you can't *possibly* understand.'

'Point taken.' The detective chief inspector nodded, glumly. 'Nevertheless, you can't really expect me to *approve*.'

'Not officially,' agreed the man.

'I've spoken to your daughter,' murmured the detective chief inspector.

'What?' The man seemed startled.

'As soon as you mentioned the kidnapping.' The detective chief inspector smiled. 'I *didn't* go out for cigarettes. That was a ploy, I'm afraid. I always keep a couple of spare packets in my desk drawer.'

The man looked angry, and began, 'You said you had to . . .'

'*You* say you've poisoned your wife, my friend.' The detective chief inspector was no longer smiling. 'I've been listening to one hell of a story. *Something* had to be verified, as soon as possible.'

'And?'

'Something *has* been verified.'

'What?'

'The kidnapping bit. Her story tallies with yours.'

'Did you think it wouldn't?'

'I'll tell you what I *do* think,' said the detective chief inspector, mildly. 'I think that, had I been in *your* shoes, I'd have asked a few more questions.'

'From Jenny? From my wife?'

'From *somebody*. This mysterious party, from where your daughter was abducted, for example. Where was it held?'

'I don't know.'

'You didn't ask?'

'No.'

'Why not?'

'It might have put Jenny's life in jeopardy.'

'*After* she'd returned home?'

'You speak with all the wisdom of hindsight, Chief Inspector,' said the man, smoothly.

'Less than a fortnight after she'd been abducted?'

'I was still worried about her safety. For months – years – I was tormented by the possibility that the kidnapping might be repeated.'

'Or that *you* might be in trouble for not reporting the kidnapping in the first place?' suggested the detective chief inspector.

'That, too, might have had a bearing upon my decision,' admitted the man.

'Did you ask Jenny?'

'What?'

'About that fateful party? About where it was held? About who was there?'

'No. We took that part of her life and refused to even acknowledge it had happened. It seemed best.'

'Best?'

'For Jenny. To help her forget. To help her recover.'

'She was shocked?'

'Of course she was shocked.' The man sounded indignant. 'She'd been kidnapped. She'd been— '

'She didn't *seem* unduly shocked,' interrupted the detective chief inspector.

'When?'

'When I spoke to her, earlier. She wasn't particularly communicative, but she certainly wasn't *shocked*.'

'It's some time ago now, of course.'

'Of course.'

'She can talk about it.'

'Has she ever been *encouraged* to talk about it?'

'No.' The man's answer was awkward rather than evasive. He continued, 'The habit grew, you see. The habit of never mentioning the subject.'

'A bad habit,' mused the detective chief inspector.

'It seemed wise at the time.'

'Nevertheless a bad habit . . . like murdering your wife.'

Had Jenny not been silly enough to marry this Walter character, Norah might still be alive. With my daughter as an ever-present sheet-anchor I doubt if I would have been driven to poisoning my wife.

Understand me. That is neither an excuse nor a shifting of the blame. I give it as a simple statement of convinced opinion; that with Jenny – especially with the *real* Jenny – I could have tolerated Norah indefinitely.

And Jenny, undoubtedly, *was* recovering.

She was reverting back to the daughter I'd known before the kidnapping. The smile was coming quicker and with less effort. The cheeks were becoming less pale. She began visiting my study again. Just the two of us, recapturing some of that warm closeness I valued so much.

She even started going out with her friends again. Not as often as before, and never late home. Always with my full permission, but with the strict proviso that she never left the side of somebody in whom she had complete trust.

That kidnapping had a curious boomerang effect upon my marriage.

For those few days when we waited for news, Norah and I had almost grown close. It was not a re-flowering of love. Nothing as dramatic as that. Merely that for those few days we conversed without bitterness. We actually *spoke* to each other.

It was, I suppose, a bond of mutual worry.

But shortly after she and Jenny returned home the refrigerative atmosphere worsened until it reached a new low. We were less communicative than strangers passing in the street. We each made believe the other didn't even exist.

The place was kept clean. The laundry and general housework could not be faulted. There was a meal waiting each evening when I returned to the bungalow, but there was a complete absence of touch or mutual interest.

The women's groups weren't enough. She now turned to

110

amateur dramatics. Not to act, but to be one of the dogsbodies who fetch and carry, or pull ropes or flick switches on cue.

Anything to get out of the house. Not to be there when *I* was there.

It became no hardship – indeed, it became the norm – for us to go for days without speaking to each other. Without even consciously noticing that the other was alive.

Nor did it worry me.

I had my own world, encompassed by the shop and the study, and it was a sufficiently wide enough world for my taste. I had my stamps, I had my books, I had my music and, most important of all, I had Jenny. I didn't *need* anybody else.

Almost shyly at first, but with growing confidence, she came back to me. As well as visiting me in the study, as Norah's outside interests grew, we had the whole house in which to wander; a kitchen in which to sip hot chocolate, a well-furnished sitting room in which to watch television shows of our choice.

I was so sure we were complete. So sure we didn't need anybody else.

And I was so wrong!

The man, Walter, was a 'representative'. A 'commercial traveller'. A lickspittle type who had taken over from one of the regular reps, and who visited the shop one afternoon in an attempt to fill his order book.

He wasn't even a *young* man. He was fifteen years older than Jenny, and he'd been divorced. Jenny, of course, insisted that it was *he* who had done the 'divorcing' – that he was the so-called injured party – but, to me, that made no difference. He was shop-soiled. He was second-hand. He hadn't even been able to make *one* marriage work.

I didn't know this, of course. Not that first day he visited the shop. I learned all that later. On *that* day, the only thing I

111

knew was that he was a newcomer to the job. That he was very unsure of himself, but that he represented the manufacturers of certain toiletries that enjoyed a steady sale. He was necessary – a necessary irritation – in order for me to stock my shelves.

He'd been there less than thirty minutes when Jenny called at the shop. She waited patiently until I'd completed my order then, as was customary, I invited this rep – this Walter – to join me in a cup of tea, while he made up his order book. It seemed natural enough to suggest that Jenny come with us to the tiny office at the rear of the dispensary.

The assistant brought the tea, and good manners insisted that I make introductions.

'This is my daughter, Jenny.'

'Nice to meet you, Miss.'

'Jenny,' she smiled.

'My name's Walter.'

Very hurriedly, I explained, 'This gentleman has replaced one of the other travellers.'

'He's been moved to another area.' It was an unnecessary explanation, but the Walter character made it sound both interesting and important.

'Where are *you* from?' asked Jenny.

'Lincolnshire. A market town called Horncastle.'

I was more than a little surprised – *and* slightly annoyed – when Jenny showed real interest in the man's past. There was much talk of 'Yellow-bellies', of poaching and of sugar beet.

'And Five Bomber Group,' he enthused. 'It was known, in the war, as 'Bomber County', Lancaster bombers all over the place.'

'Before your time,' I reminded him.

'But it must have been very exciting.' Jenny's eyes fairly sparkled as she made the remark.

'Father flew with Five Group,' he boasted. 'It's where he met Mother. After the war they settled in Lincolnshire.'

I had to leave them, to make up prescriptions, but I did so with some trepidation. He'd come to sell me soap and talc and that, in my personal opinion, was the sum total of his worth.

That evening Jenny went out with a 'friend'. Singular – not 'friends' – although at the time I thought little about it.

That, I think, is what hurt. The mild deception. The fact that she must have realised that I would have disapproved and, therefore, chose to let me remain ignorant.

Nevertheless, when she returned home she visited me in the study and, from pure paternal interest, I asked her how things had gone.

'Lovely.' Her enthusiasm was of a degree I hadn't seen since before the kidnapping, and it pleased me. She added, 'We had a lovely time, Daddy. We've arranged to meet again, on Tuesday evening.'

'We?'

'The two of us. Walter and me.'

'Do I know him?' I smiled as I asked the question. My innocence was such that, at that moment, the name meant nothing to me.

'Of course. You introduced us to each other this afternoon.'

'You mean . . .' I think I gaped.

'We went to see *Paris, Texas*.'

'Paris where?'

'*Paris, Texas*. It's a film. A wonderful film. It's about this man who's lost his memory, and . . .'

'That rep! That commercial *traveller*!'

'Daddy, don't be so pompous.'

I picked up the newspaper and riffled through the pages.

I said, 'I don't see it advertised. This film you say you've been to see. I don't see it . . .'

'It was a Film Society showing, at Preston.'

'*Preston!*'

'That's where it was being shown.' She stared, as if unable to understand the reason for my annoyance. 'It's not the sort of film you can see at any old cinema. It's a very *special* film. That's why we went. Then we called for a drink and a snack at a country pub on the way back.'

'With this "Walter" person?' I choked.

'Of course.'

'Dammit, child,' I exploded, 'you don't *know* the man.'

'I'm not a child.' She pouted and, for the first time in her life, matched anger with anger. 'You've told me *that* too many times for me to have any doubts.'

'You're *my* child.' I fought to control myself. The last thing I wanted was a slanging match with Jenny. 'As long as you live, and however old you are, you'll always be *my* child.'

'I've had a lovely evening.' She made the words sound like a flung-down gauntlet. 'And now you're spoiling it all.'

'You don't *know* the man,' I repeated.

'I know he's kind. I know he's good. And I know he's not at all like the rest of the crowd I knock about with.'

'He's much older, of course,' I sneered.

'*You're* older.'

'And no doubt he's married . . . and don't say *I'm* married.'

'Divorced, if you must know.'

'Yes, I think I "must" know. And children?'

'No children . . . if that means anything.'

'And doesn't it?'

'Not to me. He divorced his wife, because she was the wrong woman for him.'

'She didn't "understand" him?' I mocked.

'Basically.'

'Good God!'

'And what does *that* mean?'

'That approach was old when *I* was your age.'

'Therefore it doesn't happen?'

'All I'm saying is—'

'Does Mummy "understand" *you*?' Her rage broke, like a sudden thunderstorm.

'That's not quite the same . . .'

'Don't *you* wish you'd never met *her*?'

'Jenny! I'll not allow you to . . .'

'You can't pull the wool over *my* eyes, you know. I've lived here all my life . . . remember? Therefore, of all people, not *me*.'

And with that she flounced from the study and left me speechless but without real counter-argument.

I sat alone, and wished. I wished I could have held up my own marriage as an example of unqualified success. I wished I could have convinced Jenny that creatures like this Walter person were not for her. I wished I could find some way in which to show her of her importance to me. Of the vast emptiness of my life if she should ever move away from me.

I wished so many things, and I was afraid.

To say I continued to be upset would be an understatement. Nor did the fear leave me. Jenny was part of my own very limited world. Indeed, only Jenny had been allowed into that world, for more years than I cared to remember.

I had, you see, a terrible premonition. A dark and bitter feeling that something terrible was about to happen.

It was far more than the feelings of a father who sees his daughter concentrating her attentions upon another man. More than the natural belief of every father that no man is *quite* good enough for *his* daughter. It was much more than that.

I knew what the man was. I knew his kind. Every week I met them in the shop. I knew *exactly* what he was.

He had no future. He was a fool, subjected to the whims and requirements of shopkeepers. A hawker of pomades and beautifiers. A creature dependent on the success or failure of unknown PR men. Unsafe. Unsure. A mere pedlar in falsifications.

Over the years I had known these 'representatives'. I had known too many of them, and I had known them too well.

They carry a fund of risqué jokes in their heads while they, in turn, have long been the object of such jokes. Their reputation is deserved. They hawk themselves as they hawk their products. That is the basis of all salesmanship. 'First, sell yourself.'

And that was what had happened to Jenny. A man too old to be her husband had used the skills of his occupation and 'sold' himself to *her*.

He had waited until I was absent before wheedling a meeting with her. He had taken her miles from Rogate-on-Sands to see some cinema show. He had fed her a 'selling line' which insisted that although he was divorced he was also 'innocent'.

In short, he had tricked her, and, moreover, tricked her successfully enough to make her reject the advice from the only man who placed *her* happiness above all else.

It was Norah who told me they were to be married.

Norah! Jenny – *my* Jenny – had been turned against me. This man with whom she was besotted had changed her as much as *that*. She could no longer face me and tell me of the most important decision in her life.

'She's entitled to happiness,' said Norah.

'She'll certainly not be happy with him.'

Our own married life had become little more than the occasional exchange of necessary remarks; 'conversation', as such, had long since ceased. At least half my home life was spent in the solitude of my study, and a large slice of Norah's life was spent *away* from home. We had honed the skill of sharing the bungalow – of being aware that we lived under the same roof – to an absolute minimum.

But now we conversed. We even argued with some degree

116

of passion. Our battlefield was our daughter and, like all married couples when they clash, head-on, we neither gave nor expected quarter.

'She told *you*,' I'd raged. 'That clown she claims to love has changed her. He's made her sly. Underhand. Instead of telling me, she's seen fit to tell *you*!'

'Aren't you forgetting something?' she'd asked, coldly.

'What?'

'I'm her mother. Who else should she tell, if not her mother?'

'Damnation, I'm close to her. All her life, I've been close to her.'

'Apparently not as close as you thought.' The thin smile of triumph had been dagger-sharp.

'Closer than *you*.'

'It would seem not.'

'I was entitled to know.'

Then Norah had said, '*She's* entitled to happiness.'

The certainty with which she'd made the remark staggered me. We were in the kitchen. I'd been surprised to find Norah still in the bungalow on my return from the shop, but she'd left me alone until I'd finished the meal, then she'd come into the kitchen to tell me.

And now she'd made that particularly senseless remark.

I stared at her, dumbfounded. I couldn't accept that she was serious.

I almost snarled, 'She'll certainly not be happy with *him*.'

'You think not?'

'Happiness!' I gasped. 'You think the moronic lout she's befriended can give our daughter *happiness*?'

'More than "befriended".'

'More's the pity.'

'Herbert . . .' Perhaps there was something akin to sadness in the carefully controlled tone. 'What can *we* hold up as an example of "happiness"?'

* * *

There was much else along the same lines. I had thought it impossible for Norah to hurt me and, equally, impossible for me to hurt her. I was proved wrong. By using Jenny as the conduit for our respective fury, we could each drive the knife as deeply as ever.

We ended because we'd each run out of insults. Like two bruisers who had fought themselves to a standstill. Panting a little. Each carrying marks we'd wear for the rest of our lives.

Then she turned on her heel and left the kitchen, and I rose from the table and walked slowly to the sanctuary of my study.

I did not go to the wedding.

I made no excuse. I saw no reason to forgive *or* forget and, had I been tempted, the clash I'd had with Norah removed the possibility of any last-minute change of mind.

I contacted those who employed the son-in-law I did not want and cancelled all orders. I told them I did not wish to see their representative at my shop again. I gave no reason; it was none of their business. The truth is, I wanted that marriage to fail, and as soon as possible. I wanted Jenny to come to her senses.

Vicious? Vindictive? Spiteful?

I can appreciate that, discounting the circumstances leading to that marriage, those are the accusations likely to be levelled. But those circumstances can *not* be discounted.

I had loved Jenny too long, and too much. I had given her far too much of myself for me to remain passive when another man snatched her from my protection.

I wanted her back, and I was prepared to do anything – *anything!* – to get her back.

IX

The detective chief inspector knew from experience that listening could be very tiring. To really *listen*. To hear every word and catch every inflexion. Every modulation and every emphasis. To know what the speaker was really *saying*. Not just the mouthing – not even what the speaker *thought* he was saying – but what he was *really* saying.

'Certain contradictions.' He killed a yawn as he made the observation and, as he raised a hand, he glanced at his watch. The long, thin small-hours were moving into their stride. He loosened his tie as he added, 'Certain aspects. They don't quite dovetail.'

'In what I've said?' The man looked genuinely surprised.

'In your story.' The detective chief inspector scratched a thumb-nail meditatively across the hint of stubble at the side of his jaw. 'As you've told it.'

'There shouldn't be. It's the truth.'

'Your truth.' The detective chief inspector spoke with restrained patience. He raised his hand higher and rubbed his forehead, as if erasing a tiredness which had not yet reached his eyes. He smiled and said, 'At best, the truth as you see it. Or as you want *me* to see it.'

119

'There's only one "truth",' protested the man.

'My friend,' sighed the detective chief inspector. 'The nearest any of us ever get to the truth boils down to a firmly held conviction.'

'The sun will rise tomorrow,' smiled the man. 'That is an undeniable truth.'

'*Your* sun?' countered the detective chief inspector.

'I don't follow.'

'If you're not around to see it, it won't rise.'

'Hair-splitting!' The man's smile broadened as he made the remark.

'One morning your wife's sun didn't rise,' insisted the detective chief inspector. 'It won't rise again.'

'But *the* sun?'

'Now who's splitting hairs?' The detective chief inspector leaned forward. He rested his forearm on the table, then, very solemnly, said, 'You've gone too far. You've said too much.'

'I've told the truth.' The man's voice was as sombre as that of the detective chief inspector.

'I'll hear the rest.' It was a pleasantly spoken invitation. It was almost friendly in that it carried no hint of threat. 'It's what I'm paid for, my friend. What I'm good at. You talk, I'll listen. Then we'll have a break – a snack, perhaps – and I'll reach my decision. Whether *your* truth tallies with *my* truth.'

120

I think it was probably the strain of the wedding and the preparation for the wedding. Women take these things so seriously. It may have been that my refusal to attend the wedding added something to the strain. I accept that I may not be without fault.

Equally, there was an increase in the activity with Norah's various women's groups. There seemed not to be enough hours in the day, and she seemed to become more and more involved.

On the other hand, these things happen. No doctor can put his finger on the exact cause.

For whatever reason, she suffered two heart attacks in the course of a year.

Neither was more than a moderate affair. I think they frightened her but, to give credit where due, she seemed remarkably composed on the two times I visited her in the intensive-care unit. She was, of course, pale. Her hair was in some disarray. With tubes leading to various pieces of equipment, she no doubt looked worse than she was.

Each time, she stayed in intensive-care for forty-eight hours, was then moved into a main ward and was back home within a fortnight.

Thereafter the GP called in twice a week and insisted that she take life more sedately for a time. Jenny visited during the day, while I was away at the shop, and tidied the house before preparing a meal for my return, but she made sure we never actually met. Marital vows insisted that I take as much care as was reasonable while I was at home, but I think Norah resented whatever it was I did. In truth, I didn't fuss too much. At her weakest, I helped her to undress – helped her into and out of the bath – but it was not for love. It was the sort of thing one might do for an exhausted pigeon; feed it, water it and wait until it gathers enough strength to fend for itself.

If that is compassion, then I was compassionate. But I think I'd have done the same for a stranger.

In retrospect, for about two years we lived a strange life. Unreal, even by our unusual yardstick.

I still slept in my own bedroom but, when she was at her worst, I kept the doors between our respective bedrooms wide open in case she called. It was inconvenient, but it was the least I could do.

Friends visited her during the day, but they'd left by the time I arrived home each evening. Gradually, after each of the two attacks, she gained strength and eventually those same friends called to take her to her various women's groups, then brought her home afterwards. Sometimes I had a light supper ready and on those occasions we talked a little.

Hints were dropped – no more than hints – that Jenny and I should make up our differences. That the man who had taken Jenny from me was turning out to be a good husband, despite my previously held opinion. Mere hints, you understand, therefore I ignored them.

I wanted Jenny back where she belonged. Of course I did! But she'd made a choice and it was a stupid choice, therefore *she*, not Norah, was the one to meet me and admit her mistake.

Meanwhile the GP insisted upon checking Norah's progress every ten days or so. We'd known him years, and he seemed anxious. I suppose he had cause to be. Cardiac problems, while not the killers they once were, rarely come singly and, quite often, they *can* be fatal. At best they can be an inconvenience both for the patient and for those responsible for caring for the patient.

That, then, brings me to the day the sunglasses were stolen from the shop. The day when I realised that I was seriously contemplating poisoning my wife.

Aconitine. Or, if you like, aconite.

I am prepared to agree that the unaccustomed fluster brought about by the heart attacks effectuated my decision to murder Norah, but I insist that the decision was already *there*, hidden away in my subconscious. It surfaced on one particular day. I acknowledged its existence when my fingers touched the poison cabinet.

The decision as to the poison was reached, and I needed very little. The textbooks assured me that four grains of the extract was sufficient, and that death could be expected within eight hours, after giddiness, unconsciousness and cardiac or respiratory failure.

The task of administering the poison was simple. The GP had prescribed pentaerythritol for Norah's heart condition and chlordiazepoxide to steady her nerves. Both were in capsule form. I merely opened the appropriate capsules, substituted aconitine for their original contents, bottled and labelled the doctored capsules and switched bottles while she was at one of her groups.

She took the poison herself.

That night, when I retired, I locked the door of my study. I also closed my bedroom door.

By next morning I was a widower.

I replaced the genuine bottles of capsules, then telephoned the GP. He arrived within the hour. He commiserated, after verifying that she was dead, and completed a death certificate showing death as being due to heart failure.

After he'd left I needed a drink. It was unusual, at that hour, but in truth it was an unusual day. I was trembling a little. Perhaps a reaction. Perhaps with relief. It had been so *easy*!

At that moment, I almost believed in fate. The heart attacks. The GP who had been half-expecting another, and possibly fatal, coronary. The capsules that had been so easy to doctor. If not fate, what else? All I'd done was take advantage of circumstances as they'd arisen.

Jenny was upset. This was to be expected, but she was far more upset than I thought she might be. I'd waited until I was reasonably sure that moronic husband of hers had left the house, then I'd telephoned and she'd rushed round to the bungalow immediately.

She seemed mildly outraged that I was not openly distraught.

'You're taking it very calmly.' It was almost an accusation.

'I'm not over-emotive.'

The slight tightening of the mouth corners called me a liar.

'It was half-expected,' I insisted. 'She could have died on the two other occasions.'

'You weren't with her?'

'No.' I kept my voice steady and the answer short.

'Shouldn't you have been?'

'Had I known . . .' I moved my shoulders.

I could not understand her quiet determination to apportion blame. It worried me. It was a part of her character that her marriage had exposed, and it wasn't nice. It made her hard. Brittle. Not the Jenny I'd once known so well.

'Did she call?' she asked.

'What?'

'In the night. Did she call?'

'No.'

'Would you have *heard* her?'

'Of course,' I lied. 'The doors were open and as you know I'm a light sleeper.'

'She just died,' she said, heavily.

'In her sleep.'

'Just like that.'

Very gently I said, 'It's the best way to go, pet.'

Her tone had held no suspicion. As far as Jenny was concerned, her mother had died of a heart attack. She was, I think, a little concerned that she'd died alone, but her pique was based upon nothing more than that.

As for me, I felt no guilt, therefore I had no need to make pretence and hide guilt. Norah's life had not been a happy life and, had she been given a choice, I think she might have approved of what I had done. She was out of her prolonged but self-inflicted misery. I had, therefore, done her an indirect kindness.

There followed a short bout of tears and a wistful look at her dead mother before Jenny blew her nose, then went to the kitchen to brew strong, sweet tea.

Odd. It was our first meeting since she had married but other than the strained atmosphere brought about by her mother's death there was no awkwardness. No apology had been offered and, under the circumstances, I didn't press for one. I was content in the knowledge that Jenny still loved me, and I wished things to return to their previous state.

We sat in the lounge and sipped tea. Jenny took a packet of cigarettes from her handbag and lighted one.

'Something else he's taught you?' I nodded at the smoking cigarette.

She ignored the gentle criticism and, in a low voice, asked, 'Can you manage?'

'What?'

'The arrangements. The funeral arrangements.'

'Of course.' The question surprised me.

There was a pause, then she said, 'What do you intend doing?'

Again, the question puzzled me.

'Burial or cremation?' she asked, in a sad voice.

'Cremation,' I said, firmly. 'Your mother was a great believer in cremation, and the scattering of the ashes.'

'Scattering?' She frowned. 'Where?'

'The Lake District.'

'Why on earth . . .?'

'Specifically, Ullswater.'

'Why *Ullswater*?'

'It has memories,' I said, and it was no less than the truth.

'Oh!' She did not press the point and, after a moment, she asked, 'What about Grandma and Grandad?'

'I think you should telephone them,' I suggested. 'If it's

125

too far for them to travel, tell them we'll understand.'

'Oh, I think they'll come.'

'Perhaps.'

Norah's parents did not attend the funeral. They were elderly, and perhaps the journey *was* a little too much for them to undertake. Equally, I hadn't seen them since they'd moved south, and they knew I had no feelings for them.

It was a quiet cremation. Quiet, quick and conveyor-belt-like in its efficiency. Jenny, myself and a scattering of Norah's friends waited in an uncomfortable ante-room pending the conclusion of the service scheduled to be performed prior to Norah's. As we left the ante-room the mourners for the cremation following Norah's entered to await their turn.

It was all very organised and cold-blooded.

It was a 'No Flowers by Request' ceremony and that, too, added to the starkness. Some cleric we didn't know mouthed a passage from the Bible in a bored and plummy voice, then the coffin moved silently to its place in the queue behind drawn curtains.

Two days later I collected the ashes.

They were in the same sort of plastic bag, and I drove north and took a boat onto the waters of Ullswater. The same dark, rippling waters. The same stain, which sank and disappeared from sight.

But this time it meant nothing.

It meant nothing at all.

That was little more than a year ago.

I have learned many truths in this last year. It has, I think, been the most unhappy year of my life. A long, dreary, lonely year. A year of indescribable sorrow.

Perhaps I was too optimistic. Too sure. Too confident of the strength of love that bound Jenny and myself together.

I expected her to return. To take her previous place in my life. To become 'my' Jenny again.

She didn't.

126

She didn't even visit me. I have not seen her since the funeral of her mother.

This I place squarely at the door of the scoundrel she married. How he did it, God knows, but he turned her against me. A year ago, I would have counted it a near-impossibility. She *would* return. Given time, she *would* come to her senses and see in me the one person who had ever truly loved her.

Not so!

It follows, therefore, that if I have ever hated anybody in my life, that creature is the man who married my daughter. Him, and nobody else. Not Norah. I did *not* hate Norah.

Indeed, I have missed my wife more than I would have thought possible.

Of course we were not 'close' or, come to that, ever had been. We were not 'fulfilled' – not 'complete' – if by such vague expressions the meaning is that beloved of romantic ninnies who slobber their mock-emotions in cheap novels. But we *were* each a part of the other's life. Vital to each other.

It is said that loneliness is dark. Even black. Not so! Loneliness has no colour. It has no shape, no sound . . . no *anything*. It cannot be described. It can only be experienced.

Gradually – painfully – I learned how much I missed Norah. For as long as I could remember we hadn't slept together. For years we had never even made pretence of being man and wife in the accepted sense of the word. And yet she had been part of my life.

Had Jenny returned to me, I might have coped. With the knowledge I now possess – the knowledge of hindsight – I realise that even with Jenny to help it would have been difficult.

Without Jenny, it was impossible.

Therefore . . . conscience? Guilt, perhaps?

It is hard to say. I am too close, too involved and my judgement is far too subjective. All I know is that in killing

127

Norah I did myself an irreparable hurt, and that I have lived with that hurt for more than a year. Somehow, I need to cleanse myself of that hurt.

I cannot hope for forgiveness. But I need peace.

THE TENTH INTERVIEW

Detective Chief Inspector Lyle. A slightly off-putting man in that his frame seemed to be a size too large for his body. He was all angles and corners; a general mess of joints and bone-ends that looked as if they might burst a way through his skin at any moment. Not a handsome man but at least not run-of-the-mill. He was tall and at first sight gave the impression of being gaunt almost to the point of emaciation, but that was an optical illusion. His was the awkward gauntness of the cheetah; the inelegance of controlled power ready to explode into action.

His eyes were unusual in that their colour was of pure, forget-me-not blue. Despite their sheen, they were not hard eyes, but they *were* piercing and, to those who knew him, epitomised their owner's ability to flense falsehood until only the bones of bare truth remained.

The pharmacist, Herbert Grantley, had never encountered anybody like Lyle before. His own tendency towards arrogance – born, as it was, of the unconscious pomposity of the successful small-businessman – obviously had no effect upon the detective chief inspector. It neither disquieted Lyle nor intimidated him.

Indeed, during the break for something to eat and drink, Lyle hadn't once mentioned the reason for Grantley's visit to Rogate-on-Sands police station. The conversation had been about books and music; subjects upon which Grantley had been surprised by the depth of understanding shown by the detective chief inspector.

And, as Lyle led the way from the tiny canteen, Grantley realised that they were not returning to the Interview Room. Instead, they ended up in Lyle's own office, with Lyle relaxing in a spring-backed swivel-chair behind his desk and Grantley, equally relaxed, in a comfortable enough wing-chair the desk-width away.

'So many questions.' The remark rode upon what was almost a chuckle as Lyle leaned sideways, opened one of the lower drawers of the desk and took out a foolscap pad. He closed the drawer, placed the pad on the otherwise bare surface of the desk, then slipped a slim, gold-plated ballpoint from the inside pocket of his jacket. He added, 'Too many questions to remember all the answers,' then asked, 'The name is Grantley . . . right? Herbert Grantley, pharmacist. Or do you prefer to be called a chemist?'

'A pharmacist,' said Grantley.

Lyle wrote on the narrow-ruled lines of the foolscap as he talked. His handwriting was tiny and neat and he did not raise his head as he asked the questions and received the answers.

'You claim to have killed your wife?'

'That's why I'm here.'

'Murdered her?'

'Of course.'

'Specifically, poisoned her?'

'I've already told you. By means of aconitine.'

'That was a year ago?'

'About a year.'

'You've lived with it for a year? The knowledge, I mean? The guilt, if you like?'

'I can't live with it any longer.'

'Meaning, it was a mistake?'

'I didn't *poison* her by mistake. That was a very deliberate decision.'

'But a mistaken decision?'

'I now know it to be such.'

'The realisation has taken twelve long months?' Lyle tapped his chin gently with the ballpoint as he asked the question.

'One has to be driven to make the sort of confession *I've* made.'

'A very long drive. Or, perhaps, not a very *fast* drive.'

'I'm sacrificing my liberty, Chief Inspector.'

'Not yet,' murmured Lyle. 'Not yet, Grantley. A court of law, not a policeman, reaches *that* decision.'

'I have no intention of pleading—'

'The kidnapping,' interrupted Lyle. Without raising his head he stared at Grantley from beneath his brows. 'Why you?'

'I beg your pardon?' The unexpected question had caught Grantley wrong-footed.

'Why you?' repeated Lyle. 'Why Jenny?'

'I'm sorry. I don't . . .'

'You're not a well-known personality. Not a pop star. Not the richest man in Rogate-on-Sands . . . or are you?'

'No. Of course not.'

'Which raises the question. Why *you*? Why *your* daughter?'

'They – they knew how much I thought about her?' suggested Grantley. 'They knew I'd pay.'

'"They"?'

'The kidnappers.'

'Accepting that . . . which I don't,' drawled Lyle, 'how did "they" know you *could* pay?'

'Ten thousand pounds?' There was a hint of contempt in Grantley's counter-question.

'Not a lot?' Now it was Lyle's turn to counter-question.

'Chief Inspector, I own my own business.'

'A precarious business, though.'

'I don't see how you can . . .'

'I can't. You *have*,' said Lyle, gently. 'The chain-store chemists . . . remember? The argument you put to your wife. Independent pharmacists are going bust every day. One of *them* couldn't have written off ten thousand too easily.'

'In such circumstances, they'd have found it . . . surely?'

'On the other hand,' teased Lyle, 'you're quite right.'

'I'm sorry. I don't . . .'

'Ten thousand. Very poverty-stricken kidnappers.'

'You can't have it both ways, Chief Inspector,' smiled Grantley.

'I don't want it *either* way.' Lyle raised his head and the blue eyes contradicted the smile still hovering on Grantley's lips. 'You handed it to me on a plate, my friend. I didn't *ask* for it. It was served up, and it was messy, and it's still messy.'

'Messy?'

'Very messy,' insisted Lyle. 'A snatch from a party. A party to which she'd no invitation. They gate-crashed that party, Grantley. She doesn't even know who *gave* the bloody party. It was one of these anything-goes, anybody-can-come affairs and, at the last minute, your daughter and her friends decided to give it a try. And, from *that* party, she was kidnapped.'

'That's what we were told,' muttered Grantley.

'And you believed it?'

'Of course. We'd no reason to disbelieve it.'

'Some organisation!' mocked Lyle.

'If – if they took advantage of a ready-made situation.' It was a suggestion, but a very tentative suggestion.

'A teenage rave-up,' insisted Lyle. 'Pop music. Booze. Hot-shot petting. Drugs.'

'I wouldn't know about that.'

'*I* would,' countered Lyle. 'Your daughter told me. And in this general cloud-nine shambles up pops a middle-aged square. Very paternal. Very understanding. Your daughter takes something of a shine to him, and he just *happens* to be the snatch man out to kidnap her. That I do *not* believe.'

Lyle gave Grantley time enough to assimilate what had been said. He stared across the table at the perplexed pharmacist while he removed a cigarette from its packet, lighted it, then reached into one of the desk drawers and placed a heavy glass ashtray alongside the foolscap pad.

'Messy?' he asked, gently.

'As . . .' Grantley moved his shoulders. 'As *you* put it.'

'Any other way of putting it?' Lyle inhaled cigarette smoke, and plumed the exhalation towards the ceiling.

'She *was* kidnapped,' insisted Grantley.

'She awakened in bed . . . so I'm told,' mused Lyle.

'That's what she told us.'

'Doped up to the eyeballs?'

'Yes.' Grantley nodded.

'Nurses with guttural voices. A view of the Alps through a convenient window. All it needed was Conrad Veidt, script by Eric Ambler, and you'd have had a real money-spinner on your hands.'

'Damn it, Chief Inspector.' Grantley growled the words. For the first time since he'd arrived at the police station, he showed real emotion. In a low but intense tone he said, 'I believe my daughter. Jenny doesn't tell lies.'

'No?' Lyle drew on the cigarette, and the question, 'How did she get there?' rode the smoke from his lips.

'Where?'

'The hospital . . . whatever it was?'

'I don't know. I never asked. We all wanted the whole thing to be forgotten.'

'She was just "taken"?'

'Obviously.'

'Then you received the phone call? The first phone call?'

'Yes. The day after she disappeared.'

'At home?'

'At home.' Grantley nodded.

'Therefore . . .' Lyle raised an eyebrow a fraction. 'Somebody knew the number.'

'It's in the book,' said Grantley, impatiently.

'Which brings us back, full circle. Why *you*?' Then, before Grantley could speak, 'No gutturals this time?'

'Muffled. As if . . .'

'I know. A handkerchief. But good English?'

'Good English,' agreed Grantley.

'And the second phone call? To the pub, as I recall?'

Grantley nodded.

'Y'see . . .' Lyle drew on the cigarette, then continued, 'By the time of the *second* phone call your daughter was

135

already in . . . wherever it was.'

'Austria.'

'Wherever it was,' repeated Lyle, gently.

'Chief Inspector, I don't like the way you're—'

'But the call didn't come from there,' interrupted Lyle.

'From Austria?'

Lyle nodded.

'I've already told you,' said Grantley. 'They must have been watching me. They must have seen me go into the public house, then telephoned. To make sure the phone wasn't being tapped . . . presumably.'

'One hell of an organisation,' mused Lyle.

'What?'

'Links here, in Rogate-on-Sands. Links in Austria. Private nursing homes. The wherewithal to hump the victim all the way across Europe. And the hair-trigger organisation by which they can snatch the victim from a party she didn't know she was going to, and telephone her father at a boozer he just *happens* to be visiting. One *hell* of an organisation.'

'Put that way—'

'That's the way it *was* . . . isn't it?'

'Yes. But—'

'And all for the sake of the daughter of a tin-pot provincial chemist.'

'That's putting it—'

'All for the sake of a niggerly ten thousand pounds. All that link-up. All that planning. All that expense. I doubt if they broke even.'

Grantley took a few deep breaths, as if to steady his nerves. Lyle merely watched and waited. When Grantley glanced at the packet of cigarettes on the desk top, and murmured, 'May I?' Lyle moved the packet and the matches a little closer to the pharmacist and waited until Grantley had lighted the cigarette. The striking of the match was a little clumsy and there was a distinct tremble to the cigarette as

Grantley held it between his lips.

'The truth,' said Lyle, at last. 'That's what we were talking about earlier. And the truth is you *did* withdraw ten thousand pounds from your bank. That can be verified, via bank records. That much is the truth.'

'But not the rest?' And now, Grantley was asking, not asserting. There was a hang-dog sound to the question.

'You packed it into the holdall, as instructed. After the second telephone call your wife took it in the car . . . and that's the last you saw of it. That, too, I'm prepared to accept as the truth.'

'It was ransom money,' muttered Grantley.

'You *still* believe that?'

'For God's sake, what else?'

'Fine.' Lyle gave a friendly nod of his head. '*I'm* prepared to believe it, too, when you've explained how your wife could have travelled to France, from France to Austria, from Austria to Switzerland, from Switzerland to France and back from France to the UK . . . *without a passport.*'

'Oh!'

'That, not counting the same route taken by your daughter. And don't start toying with the idea of packing-cases, Grantley. They, too, need documentation. And she wasn't in a packing-case on the return journey.'

Grantley said, 'Oh!' again, and it was little more than a whisper.

'A canal holiday.' If there was mockery in Lyle's voice, it was gentle mockery. 'Something "unusual". Something even daring. Have you ever *been* abroad, Grantley?'

'No.'

'Your wife?'

'Only when she . . .' He stopped, and his face twisted, as if in sudden pain.

'But she *didn't*, did she?'

Grantley stared at the detective chief inspector. The single, tiny shake of his head could have meant anything.

137

Disbelief. Agreement. Even apprehension at what was yet to come.

It was known as the 'Interview Technique' and every copper favoured his own variant. Lyle knew his own capabilities. Knew that the two-handed inquisition was not his style. For him it was a little like picking the seeds from a pomegranate; a slow and time-consuming exercise which, if successful, left only an empty fruit and the sour pith of factuality.

He allowed Grantley time to digest what had already been achieved. He smoked what remained of his cigarette and screwed the tab into the base of the glass ashtray before he continued.

'We can take it your wife didn't go traipsing off to the Continent,' he said quietly.

'It would seem not.' Grantley's tone was brittle.

'Nor did your daughter.'

'That too.'

'From which it follows there was no "kidnapping".'

Grantley swallowed, then repeated, 'It would seem not.'

'Money,' mused Lyle. 'Ten thousand pounds. If I have the picture in focus, you parted with that sum shortly after you arranged for your joint account to hold only a limited amount.'

Grantley nodded.

'Your wife obviously wanted money in a hurry. More money than she could take from the joint account.'

'That's one answer.' It was a reluctant admission.

'Let's accept it as *the* answer,' smiled Lyle, then added, 'For the moment.'

'A possible answer,' conceded Grantley.

'And, of course, your daughter was in on it.'

'That doesn't follow. I can't see Jenny—'

'Jenny *wasn't* kidnapped.' Lyle made the words hard and unyielding. 'All that crap about middle-aged men picking her up at unspecified parties. Austrian nurses, picture-postcard views from a window, Swiss hotels. Crap! All of it.'

Grantley's jaw muscles tightened.

'You were taken for a ride, my friend,' continued Lyle. 'They were both in it. They *had* to be.'

'I – I don't see—'

'Damnation, man! They *had* to be. Both of 'em.'

'That's awful,' breathed Grantley. 'Y'know . . . *awful*.'

'Therefore, the telephone messages,' murmured Lyle.

'What?'

'You did *receive* the two telephone messages?'

'Of course.'

'A man's voice. Muffled, but a man's voice?'

'Yes.'

'Muffled, because you might have recognised it had it *not* been muffled?' suggested Lyle.

'It's possible.'

'Only "possible"?'

'All right . . . likely.'

'Therefore, *who*?'

'How on earth do I—'

'Somebody in the swindle. Surely?'

'Obviously.'

'Somebody your wife and your daughter could trust. Surely?'

'Of course.'

'I'd say somebody in the family. Wouldn't you?'

'I can't think of . . .' Grantley stopped speaking, but left his mouth slightly open.

'A father? A grandfather?' drawled Lyle.

'But – but why should he? I mean, why *should* he?'

'Why should your wife want ten thousand pounds?' smiled Lyle. 'Why should your daughter pretend to be kidnapped? Why such a lot of things?'

'It fits,' mumbled Grantley. 'Good God, it fits.'

'A trip to Dorset. A trip to Frampton.' Lyle ticked the points off on his fingers. 'A wad of ready green stuff.

Something *you* couldn't be told about. But something your wife knew. Something her parents knew. But something that required a slightly involved cover-up.'

'I don't know.' Grantley shook his head in puzzlement. 'What you say makes sense, but I don't *know*. I don't know *why*.'

Lyle fingered a new cigarette from the packet. He played with it gently as he teased the interview forward.

'There is a reason.'

'I can't think of it.'

'Have you *given* it much thought?'

'No-o.' Grantley lowered his brows. 'I've always taken it for granted.'

'A kidnapping?'

'Of course. Why shouldn't I . . .?'

'But now you accept it *wasn't* kidnapping?'

'It – it seems unlikely.'

'A young woman,' said Lyle, softly. 'The daughter of a very stick-in-the-mud father. A mysterious absence, with her mother. A requirement of a large sum of money. She returns, after a week, looking – how did you put it? – pale and lack-lustre.'

'Not – not kidnapping?' Grantley's voice was whisper soft.

Lyle smiled, sadly, then said, 'Try abortion for size.'

'Oh my God!'

'I'm guessing . . .' Lyle placed the cigarette between his lips. He talked round it as he lighted it. 'We can check. We can let sleeping dogs lie. But—'

'No! Keep Jenny out of this.'

'— the way I read the script we have a healthy young lady, with a moderately understanding mother and very understanding grandparents. Grandparents tend to *be* more understanding. Her father – if you'll pardon the bluntness – is a pain in the crotch. The sort of creep who checks that the radio time-signal tallies with every watch and clock in sight.

'Those are the *dramatis personae*. Thereafter the plot. The

140

healthy young lady gets herself pregnant. She tells the understanding mother. Nobody dares break the news to the numbskull of a father; therefore, between them, they hatch up a little scheme whereby the father provides the loot, the healthy young lady beetles south to the grandparents, after the grandfather has telephoned a phoney message to the father. Abortion is organised, the mother joins the grandparents, the mother and the young lady return to the father and the whole escapade is wrapped around in a "kidnapping" con. Involved but at the same time simple. Grandad does the telephoning, prompted by wifey, who is in a perfect position to know exactly where hubby is at any given time.' Lyle paused, raised questioning eyebrows, then drawled, 'Do you *buy* it?'

Grantley nodded and looked sad.

He muttered, 'I *have* to buy it . . . don't I?'

'You have.' Lyle drew deeply on his cigarette. He added, 'Indeed you have. Otherwise, the other bit doesn't work . . . but *I* don't have to buy it.'

The pips were coming out of the pomegranate. The honeycomb of unhealthy-looking flesh was falling in upon itself. The firmness had been replaced, in part, by mush . . . and, for a moment, something not far removed from panic touched the back of Grantley's eyes.

'It's been quite a night,' observed Lyle, amiably. 'We've had quite a conversation, and I've listened to quite a few fairy stories.'

'I don't see what you mean. I came in here to . . .'

'Of course,' nodded Lyle. 'But let's go slowly. Don't let's slam it into over-drive too quickly.'

Grantley waited.

'Let's talk about *you*,' suggested Lyle. 'The wheels and springs and pawls that make *you* tick over.'

'I really don't see what . . .'

'An only child. Pampered a little . . . that at a guess. But

141

more of a pal than a son to your father. Especially when you joined him in the shop.'

'Look, I've already told you—'

'Not one of the "boys of the village". Something of a swot but, at the same time, a romantic. Reading a lot. Acquiring as much knowledge about life as possible, but once removed, as it were. Not getting out there and *experiencing* it.'

'I really can't see what you're—'

'You meet this girl. This Norah.' Lyle seemed to be talking to himself. Tabulating facts and possibilities. It was one more 'Interview Technique'. Not listening. Not questioning. But, instead, driving ahead and, in a subtle way, *re*-creating the man at whom the conversation was being aimed. He continued, 'Like yourself, an only child. Like yourself, a little spoiled, but not without intelligence. She was a romantic, too.'

'I don't see how—'

'"The Golden Road to Samarkand". I like that line. Not that I'm given much to poetry, but even *I* know that line. They tell me it isn't, though. The old camel-route to Samarkand, I mean. Very dirty. Very grimy. Shit-order every inch of the way. That's what they tell me . . . those who've seen it. But it's a nice line. Very romantic, and very appropriate for two teenagers, fed to the gills with poetic theory.'

'Chief Inspector, if you're trying to—'

'I'm trying to understand you. I'm trying to fill in a few gaps.' Lyle sounded hurt. Almost offended. 'You trot in here, keep me out of my bed, feed me a yarn about a fake kidnapping and expect me to show no depth of interest. Grantley, I need to know what sort of a lunatic I'm dealing with.'

'You're blunt.' Grantley reached forward and, without asking, helped himself to a cigarette and matches. 'All I wanted was for you to—'

'You wanted me to believe you. I *know* that. You wanted

142

me to sit here, like an official numbskull, and accept every word you uttered. No way! I'm a policeman, Grantley, not a priest. I'm not paid to accept confessions at face value, then dish out penitence. I'm paid to *disbelieve*.'

'To reach your own conclusions?' The question had a bitter ring.

'To reach the *right* conclusions.'

'For example, that I'm what you're pleased to call a "romantic"? You think *that*? Is that one of the— '

'Two teenagers,' interrupted Lyle. 'Two teenagers watching a sunset. One of 'em – the boy – quotes Flecker, and the girl understands. They're in tune with each other. Neither of 'em goes for the feely-for-feely-but-no-pushee-innee caper.'

'You're vulgar, Chief Inspector. You're— '

'I'm normal. My only abnormality – if you can call it that – is that I'm a copper. I've seen it all, and heard it all. My job – my profession – insists that I spend my working life up to the armpits in filth. Which, in turn, means I can recognise non-filth. I claim you were both romantics, and, dammit, that's not meant as a criticism. It's meant as a compliment.'

'You're mad. You're quite— '

'You loved your father. Right?'

'Of course I loved my father. He was the finest man I've ever— '

'I can take you to people who'd cheerfully knife their father. *And* think that was normal. People you could never understand. People I've had to *learn* to understand.' The hint of a smile touched Lyle's lips, as he added, 'The truth is, I wasn't too bloody keen on *my* father . . . but I'm not a romantic.'

Grantley drew on his cigarette, but remained silent.

Lyle said, 'Let's get back to the two teenagers. The love-birds. The romantics. OK, your father tried to warn you off marriage. Not too hard . . . but he hinted that every marriage has its hairy moments. Maybe it wasn't that he disapproved of the girl you'd chosen. You were too much like each other. Right? You both expected too much. Is that possible? To tell you – to warn you – that marriage isn't roses all the way, and that if you figured it was you were due to be dumped on your fanny with enough force to shake the whole foundation of your life. Maybe *that's* what he was trying to warn you.'

'It's – it's possible,' muttered Grantley.

'But you didn't take the warning, did you?' teased Lyle. 'The Byronic dream had too tight a hold. Schoolboy sentimentality stayed the norm. To wrap yourself in words. To dream your way through great music. Not just *part* of your world. Your *whole* world . . . or at least the only world you were prepared to acknowledge. God, you suffered! At work you sold pills and corn-plasters – condoms and contraceptive gadgets – even horse medicine . . . while at heart you were an aesthete, and always would be.'

The droop of Grantley's shoulders told their own tale. The hour of the morning was partly responsible, but it was more than that. It was a fatigue beyond mere physical fatigue and a fatigue far outreaching mere tiredness. Somewhere – at some point in the prolonged interview – something had caved in on itself. Some deep-down certainty had been removed, and it showed in his slumped posture, and it showed in the lines of emotional agony on his face.

'I . . .' He moistened his lips, made as if to raise his head, but didn't, then groaned, 'I tried to be a good husband. I swear! I did *try*.'

'To the girl you married,' agreed Lyle. 'But not to the woman she became. She changed, as all people change. Not for the worse. Not for the better. She merely grew up. You *didn't*.'

'I tried,' repeated Grantley, hoarsely.

'First you were a "daddy's boy". Then you were a "mummy's boy".' Lyle's tone was soft, but quite merciless. 'For you the sun never set. That damned "Golden Road to

Samarkand" remained. An illusion. But you couldn't accept it as an illusion. It was your "reality". The silks, the spices, the slave-girls . . . as far as you were concerned they were *there*. There, for evermore!'

'Norah thought the same. When we stood there and— '

'Norah grew up. You didn't.' Lyle rose from his chair. He loosened his tie a little as he began pacing, and his voice took on the mild disgust of a headmaster carpeting an unruly pupil. 'Grantley, you're beyond understanding. Beyond hope. You married a woman – presumably the woman of your choice – but that's *all* you did. You went through the motions. Said the appropriate words and wore the required clothes. After that . . . nothing! The basic *responsibilities* never entered your personal scheme of things.'

'I gave her a good home. I— '

'You can give a dog a "good home". A cat. A bloody tame rabbit. Food, warmth and shelter. That's all a "good home" boils down to.'

'I'm not a – a . . .'

'I know. You're not a "demonstrative man". You've told me that a dozen times already. In a dozen different ways. You are "unemotional". No love, no hate . . . no *anything*.'

'It's true. I can't help— '

'And what about your daughter?'

Grantley's head drooped a little lower and he didn't answer.

'A child. Is that it?' tormented Lyle. He paused in his pacing, leaned stiff-armed on the desk and slashed low-voiced contempt at the beaten man. 'A wife who's learned more sense than to be a never-ending slave-girl on your imaginary golden road. But now you had somebody else. Somebody young enough – impressionable enough – to be moulded into what *you* wanted. A new slave-girl. Bright and untouched. Malleable. All yours, if you could only keep her well away from the influence of a wife who'd already figured you out.

145

'*That* was the reason for the locked room, Grantley. The private world, in which make-believe and music took preference to reality. A world with only two keys . . . yours and hers. *That* was your real Samarkand, and the golden road was a door, and beyond that door a never-never-land inhabited by two people. An absurdity. A teenage dream. A stupid, ridiculous figment into which you could retreat.'

'It – it wasn't ridiculous,' muttered Grantley. 'It was beautiful. It was peaceful. It was—'

'*It was a lie!*'

'Y'know . . .' Lyle had resumed his seat. He had lighted another cigarette and, again, the switch of his tone preluded one more change of inquisitorial technique. This time, the can't-believe-it-possible ploy. The mock-amazement. The make-believe disbelief. The gentle – almost friendly – con of pseudo-incredulity. Lyle drawled, 'Y'know, Grantley, if I hadn't heard it from your own lips – if I hadn't *been* here – I wouldn't have credited it. A man of your obvious education thinking he could opt out of the world.'

'No. It wasn't that. Not quite *that*.' It was a very half-hearted protest, and Lyle ignored it.

'A man of *your* intelligence. And because his wife won't join him, he poisons her.'

'She was – she was quite insufferable. I mean—'

'Oh, come *on!*' Lyle smiled. 'She shared too little of your life to be *that*. She was hardly ever with you. Most of the time she was out learning how to make marmalade and patchwork quilts. You were either at the shop or locked away in your study. You didn't even sleep together. You didn't even share the same bedroom.'

'I tried,' breathed Grantley.

'In your own way,' conceded Lyle.

'I really tried.'

'In your own way,' repeated Lyle. 'But, at a guess, it was the *wrong* way. Now – again, at a guess – if you'd shown *her*

146

the patience you showed your daughter . . .'

He left the sentence unfinished, and there was a silence.

Then, Grantley fumbled, 'She was a child.'

'At first,' agreed Lyle.

'I . . .' He swallowed, then said, 'I *guided* her.'

'Why not "guide" her mother?'

'She wouldn't listen. She changed.'

'How *could* she listen? There was a locked door between you.'

'Chief Inspector,' said Grantley, heavily, 'you didn't know my wife. You don't understand.'

'Did you?'

'What?'

'Understand? Even try to understand?'

'You think it was all *my* fault?' The question was heavy with self-pity and bitterness.

'You're not *without* fault,' said Lyle, gently. 'You're not *faultless* . . . otherwise you wouldn't be here.'

'I came here for a purpose, Chief Inspector.' Grantley seemed to square his shoulders slightly. 'I came here to confess. To unburden myself, if you wish. To rid myself of an impossible weight of guilt.'

'Why?' asked Lyle, innocently.

Grantley raised his head, and stared.

'Why?' repeated Lyle.

'Is that a question that really *needs* an answer?'

'All questions deserve an answer.'

'Very well. Is it a question *you* need to ask?'

'Why not?'

'As a senior police officer. A man walks into your police station, wishing to clear his conscience of . . .'

'Ah!' Lyle seemed to pounce. 'So now we come to the subject of consciences? *Your* conscience, in particular?'

'I'm tired, Chief Inspector.' And, indeed, Grantley both sounded and looked tired. 'It seemed so easy. All it needed was courage. Just to walk in here, and . . .'

'And now . . . *courage?*' Lyle's voice held subtleties of unspoken meaning.

'If you think it was easy to— '

'Courage?' It was a gentle but dangerous question. Then, 'Courage? . . . or cunning?'

To the east, across the roofs of the town, the sky was gradually losing its blackness. Dawn wasn't far away, and dawn at Rogate-on-Sands was a peculiarly cold phenomenon. Cold and steely. Almost menacing. As if nature was demanding a harsh and brittle price for the promised glory of the scene to be enjoyed when the sun had completed its swing to the western horizon.

In the town itself, the pre-dawn workers gradually built up their number on the deserted streets. Policemen were joined by early-morning office cleaners. Live-out hotel staff hurried towards empty corridors and kitchens. Post Office workers walked, or cycled, towards the sorting offices. Railway employees made for the warmth of all-night buffets, waiting carriages and cabs. These were the citizens who knew Rogate-on-Sands as a cold and deserted place; a place where the wind from the Irish Sea could blur the vision with tears; a place of whipped-up sand spiralling in from the dunes.

For a few hours, especially in the autumn and winter months, Rogate-on-Sands ceased to be a slightly snooty holiday town and, instead, turned bitter and inhospitable.

The 'feel' of that inhospitability had somehow crept into Lyle's office. Dawn – a very special 'dawn' – was about to break, and the radiators of the central-heating system did nothing to counter the chill . . . which, indeed, had little to do with room temperature.

'To mould a fellow-human being,' growled Lyle. 'To create what *you* wanted, regardless of what *they* wanted. That, as I see things, was the object of the exercise.'

'Not deliberately,' protested Grantley. 'Perhaps so . . . but not *deliberately*.'

'Deliberately,' contradicted Lyle. 'Quite deliberately. First your wife, then your daughter. You failed in one, but succeeded in the other.'

'You think I *succeeded*?' There was ugly contempt in Grantley's words. 'To make her what I *wanted* her to be? When she married a no-good scoundrel not worthy enough to speak her name?'

'That was after the "kidnapping" fiasco.'

'She became pregnant, that's all. It wasn't—'

'Women don't "become" pregnant!' Quite suddenly all the play-acting was swept aside. The prolonged softening-up process had achieved its object. Lyle was all-detective-chief-inspector. The angles of his body seemed sharper. The eyes behind the spectacles hardened, and the tone of voice matched the sudden metamorphosis. He repeated, 'They don't "become" pregnant, Grantley. There's a rather important act called fornication required, before *that* happens.'

'I don't know who—'

'An important act called fornication,' repeated Lyle. 'I've seen your daughter, Grantley. I've talked to her. I listened to what you've had to say about her. I *don't* think she's some street-corner slag.'

'If you even *doubt* that, you're—'

'I *don't* doubt it.' Lyle gave Grantley no room in which to either argue or express an opinion. The night's session was nearing its close, all the nails had been carefully positioned and now they were being hammered home with a savagery and a certainty born of impassive proficiency. 'With Jenny it wasn't lust. It wasn't carnality. It wasn't even a mistake. She trusted . . . she trusted the wrong person, and she trusted him too far.'

Grantley opened his mouth, as if to say something, then closed it again.

'Mutual love . . . would you say?' Lyle invited a question.

'What?' Grantley looked puzzled, almost dazed.

'Between Jenny and the father of her unborn child?'

149

'Of course. Jenny wouldn't—'

'Jenny being part of his world? A vital part of his world?'

'Look, I don't see what—'

'Jenny being the sort of person who would not go the whole hog with *any* man. She had to be part of *his* world. A very vital part of his world.'

'I came here to confess to the murder of my wife,' choked Grantley.

'Ah, yes. Murder.' Lyle made it sound as if he'd just been reminded. He leaned forward slightly, then continued, 'Let's take things a step at a time, shall we, Grantley? Murder is the top rung of the ladder. Let's come down a couple of rungs. Past a kidnapping . . . which wasn't. Let's first handle the crime of incest. The crime of incest, committed by *you* upon your daughter.'

It was what it had all been leading up to. The cage of words which Grantley had been allowed to weave around himself; the trap he himself had constructed. And now Lyle sprang the trap and before Grantley could seek an escape he continued.

'If you're thinking of denying it, Grantley, I should warn you. I'm prepared to interview your daughter. *And* your in-laws. I'm prepared to trace whoever performed the abortion, and interview *them*. Before you call *me* a liar, be warned. I have the means – and the intention, if necessary – to prove *you* a liar.'

Grantley rubbed dry lips together, then moistened them with the tip of his tongue.

'They tell me it's one in ten.' Lyle smashed the accusation home, remorselessly. 'Ten per cent of all youngsters. By the nature of things, mostly girls. But, one in ten. And that's only the "official" figure. The get-at-able figure. The *known* number. Her father, her uncle, her elder brother – some foul bastard she's been taught to respect – takes advantage and defiles her. A touch here, a touch there. Sometimes – like

150

you – all the way.'

'I – I – I—'

'*Don't!*' Lyle brought the flat of his hand down on the surface of the desk. There was terrifying certainty in his tone, as he snapped, 'Like a jigsaw puzzle, Grantley. Tonight. That's what you've done. All that talk. All those phrases. Each faintly recognisable but, individually, meaning nothing. But put the pieces together and the jigsaw is complete. That's what you've done, Grantley . . . you've put all the pieces together.' Lyle pointed a stiffened finger and growled, 'I know what I'm looking at, Grantley. I know *exactly* what I'm looking at. I don't *like* it, but I can *recognise* it. I've seen guyed-up filth far too many times. Half my life I've had to handle bastards like you, and force myself to keep my fingers from their necks. You're not the first. You won't be the last.'

There was no shouting. No histrionics. Indeed, as Lyle moved into the tirade, his voice seemed to lower both in volume and tone. But the disgust was there. The disgust and the anger that this man, Grantley, had entered the police station convinced that he could throw dust in the eyes of professional man-hunters trained and experienced in un-covering guile.

Nor had Grantley any illusions left. The last seed was out of the pomegranate and the brittle shell was being squeezed into a shapeless mass of useless pith and rind.

'I loved Jenny.' It was little more than a whispered moan, and the impression was that it took great effort to force the words from a parched throat and past dry lips. 'I *loved* her.'

'You loved nobody.' Lyle stood up. He pushed his hands into the pockets of his trousers and paced the office. His speech was brittle and short-sentenced. The words were not opinions. They were conclusions. Stepping stones leading to a certainty and a truth. 'You loved nobody, Grantley. Nobody! Only yourself. You couldn't even make *friends* . . . much less *love* anybody.

'All that talk about celibacy. *You* weren't celibate,

151

Grantley. You had a *daughter*. God knows how you do it. You people . . . God only knows how you do it. What yarns you spin. What excuses you make. What sly lies you tell. But you justify it. To yourself. To the kids. Book-learning, perhaps.' Lyle's tone remained ice-cold, but a certain musing quality made a temporary veneer. 'The rulers of ancient Egypt . . . eh? Chapter and verse. The Pharaohs did it. Sisters marrying brothers. The emperors of Rome. Keep it in the family. Fathers sleeping with daughters, mothers sleeping with sons, brothers screwing their sisters. You're a book-man, Grantley. *You* could justify it. Even the Bible. The Old Testament. The Hebrew Patriarchs. Incest was the done thing in those days. You could justify it, Grantley. Biblical blessing on it, and a not-too-bright daughter. So easy. So *damned* easy!'

'I loved Jenny,' croaked Grantley.

' "Loved"?' The musing quality left Lyle's voice. 'Is that what you called it? Is that what you kidded her it was? When you put her in the family way, is *that* what you called it?' Lyle paused, then continued, 'She didn't love you . . . that for sure. She didn't even *trust* you. It was her mother she told. That must have been one of the high spots of your wife's life. To be told, by her daughter, that *you* had slipped a bun in the oven. My God! That must have been some moment.

'That's why they took you for a ride, my friend. Your in-laws, your wife, your daughter. Between them, they worked out the "kidnapping" stunt. To make you sweat a little. To make you squirm. And to make you unzip your purse and pay for everything. It was as clear as glass. As a con, it was a non-starter. But you were so bloody sure of yourself. So self-opinionated. So self-satisfied. Why *shouldn't* a tin-pot pill-pusher have his daughter held to ransom when that pill-pusher's name was Herbert Grantley? The *great* Herbert Grantley. You couldn't even see that!'

'I worked it out, later,' mumbled Grantley.

152

'Later?' mocked Lyle.

'Norah dropped hints. I worked it out.'

'Your wife told you.' The accusation was almost weary in its statement of what was, to Lyle, obvious. 'A man like you. Your daughter marries this Walter character. Your personal plaything isn't around any more. She's safe. Out of harm's way. Why *shouldn't* your wife tell you? Why shouldn't she gloat a little? You'd dragged her through hell, and she was human.'

'She hinted. I worked it out.'

'Enough hints,' mocked Lyle, 'and a thick-skinned, self-opinionated bugger like *you* can work things out.'

'I hated her.' The admission was almost inaudible. It came from behind tightened jaw muscles and closed teeth.

'Of course you did . . . but not as much as *she* hated *you*.'

'Oh no. Oh, no!' Grantley's shake of the head was quick and jerky. '*I* poisoned *her* . . . remember?'

Lyle returned to the desk. He did not go to the chair. Instead, he hoisted one buttock onto a desk corner, allowed one of his legs to swing free and reached for the packet of cigarettes. There was silence until he'd lighted the cigarette.

Then he asked, 'Why the hell should I do your dirty work, Grantley?'

Grantley watched his tormentor with suspicious eyes.

'Your wife had three heart attacks. The third one killed her.'

'She had *two* heart attacks. She died—'

'I can *prove* she had three. Medical records. The death certificate.'

'I've already admitted I—'

'You had her cremated, then you dumped the ashes in Ullswater.'

'That doesn't mean I didn't—'

'I ask you again.' Lyle's foot swung rhythmically as he stared down at a man he'd figuratively skinned, boned and

153

placed on a slab for minute inspection. He drew on the cigarette, as he repeated the question, 'Why the hell should *I* do your dirty work?'

'I – I don't understand.'

'Your wife's dead.' And now the words came out at an even pace. They were bare of all emotion other than contempt. They were homogeneous and constant. No rise, no fall. They teased aside the last shreds of pomposity from a man already bereft of all dignity and self-esteem. 'Your wife is dead. Heart attack or aconite, she no longer exists. More than that, she can't be exhumed. Even her ashes can't be examined. She's gone . . . completely.

'That was a year ago. You've waited a year, Grantley. A whole year. Guilt doesn't grow. That's a fallacy, beloved of romantics and flash novelists. It doesn't *grow*. It dies. If there *is* guilt – a feeling of guilt – it's there at the commission. A combination. Guilt and terror. It *can*, sometimes – rarely, but *sometimes* – drive a criminal to give himself up. But, with time, it passes. He learns to live with it. He forgets it. He even congratulates himself upon evading the consequences of his actions.

'That's the real world, Grantley. A world I know, inside out and back to front. Guilt didn't bring you here tonight. Something . . . but not guilt. Not the inability to live with the knowledge of what you've done . . . assuming, for the moment, you *did* it.

'Let me make an educated guess.' Lyle drew on the cigarette. 'A guess based upon a lot of experience, plus the knowledge of the type of man you are.

'Your wife has been dead for a year. Much sympathy. The poor little man, left to cope with things alone. What is more natural than his daughter taking him under her wing. Visiting him as much as possible. Maybe – y'know . . . coming *back* to him.

'She was, when all's said and done, his first "mistress". He was her first "lover". Why not leave this husband of hers?

154

Why not return to the original Garden of Eden . . . serpent, and all?

'That, Grantley, is my educated guess. That that's what you planned, and what you expected. And it didn't come off!'

Lyle paused, and there was a silence. It was a charged and ugly silence. The silence of defeat and at the same time the silence of a man unable to contradict. Lyle allowed the silence to grow before he continued.

Then he said, 'You want *me* to tell your daughter that you murdered her mother. That's why you're here. That's why you came, complete with a package of lies and half-truths.'

'I *did* poison her,' breathed Grantley.

Lyle allowed himself a quick, tight smile.

'I'll make a full statement, if that's what you want.'

'No . . . that's what *you* want.' Lyle squashed the cigarette into the ashtray. 'What you *don't* want is prison. A man like you, in the nick? . . . Don't push fantasy too far, Grantley. You want notoriety. You want your daughter in a witness box, being cross-examined. You want a forensic mud-slinging orgy, with *her* as one of the targets. That's what you *really* want.

'You? Let's say that – between these four walls – I'm beginning to believe you. Maybe you *did* poison your wife. If so, you've committed the perfect crime. No body. No proof. Official documentation that she died of a heart attack.

'It doesn't matter a damn what you say *now*, you'll walk out of court a free man. Before the jury retire you'll have *proved* you didn't kill her. The police will look mugs. The press will have a field day, emphasising the danger of the common man once coppers go off at half-cock. *But your daughter will know and your daughter will believe.*' Lyle hoisted himself from the desk corner and strolled towards the door. As his hand closed on the knob, he murmured, 'On your way, Grantley.'

'You – you mean . . .'

155

'Tell her yourself. Do it the easy way, if you must . . . or maybe it's the *hard* way.'

'I'll – I'll go above you, Lyle,' threatened Grantley. 'I'll go to the chief constable if necessary.'

'And he,' smiled Lyle, 'will send the file down the line to *me*. I'll read it, then return it marked "insufficient proof".'

'I *killed* her.'

'Live with it.' Lyle opened the door. There was a terrifying calmness as he added, 'If you can't live with it, you have access to enough poisons. I'll handle your suicide without wasting a single tear.'

Lyle drove home via the prom. He braked the car to a halt, then left it to stroll to the railings. It wasn't far from high tide, and the Irish Sea lapped its stone-grey waters against the base of the granite blocks that formed the foundations of the promenade.

It was cold and inhospitable. The underflow made tiny, disgusting sucking noises and the tainted foam slopped unidentifiable filth in a never-ending oscillation.

Had it been worth it? Was it *still* worth it?

Lyle couldn't decide. He'd made a decision, but it had been a decision based on the mental toss of a coin. Maybe it had been the wrong decision.

He shrugged.

It was the job, and what he was paid for. For good or evil, he made a choice. No medals if it had been the right choice, but his neck on the chopping-block if he'd been wrong.

He shrugged, turned his back on the sea and walked towards the parked car.

86-1455

F
WAI

Wainwright, John

The tenth interview

$12.95

DATE			
DEC 29 '86			